THE
GENERAL
AND JULIA

ALSO BY JON CLINCH

Marley

Finn

Kings of the Earth

The Thief of Auschwitz

Belzoni Dreams of Egypt

THE
GENERAL
AND JULIA

A Novel

JON CLINCH

ATRIA BOOKS

New York London Toronto Sydney New Delhi

ATRIA
BOOKS

An Imprint of Simon & Schuster, Inc.
1230 Avenue of the Americas
New York, NY 10020

First Atria Books hardcover edition November 2023

ATRIA BOOKS and colophon are trademarks of Simon & Schuster, Inc.

For information about special discounts for bulk purchases, please contact Simon & Schuster Special Sales at 1-866-506-1949 or business@simonandschuster.com.

The Simon & Schuster Speakers Bureau can bring authors to your live event. For more information or to book an event, contact the Simon & Schuster Speakers Bureau at 1-866-248-3049 or visit our website at www.simonspeakers.com.

Interior design by Jill Putorti

Manufactured in the United States of America

1 3 5 7 9 10 8 6 4 2

Library of Congress Cataloging-in-Publication Data has been applied for.

ISBN 978-1-6680-0978-9
ISBN 978-1-6680-0980-2 (ebook)

For Sam and Ivy

Show me a hero, and I'll write you a tragedy.

—F. SCOTT FITZGERALD

THE
GENERAL
AND JULIA

CHAPTER 1

1843

The Canary

How large a box shall be required?

The canary is the smallest of creatures, three inches long if that. To take its precise measure would be indelicate regardless of his good intentions. So he bends to it upon its bed of linen, and he touches its cool, dry, brilliant feathers with his finger, and he subtly gauges its length against the count of his knuckles. That will be measurement enough.

What is its color? The very shade of a lemon.

How much does it weigh? Little more than its own last breath.

Birdie's sudden passing breaks her heart. At sunup he was his usual cheery self, welcoming the morning to her bedroom with his repertoire of peeps and chirps and burbles. His song, his color—indeed, his very pulsing presence—were all so lovely and so familiar as to be utterly beneath notice. Now their absence pains her. His cage hangs empty, its black shadow a ragged latticework stain upon the blue wall.

Her father looks up from his soup plate, notes the little cloud of linen on the sideboard, and fixes it with a furious eye. "Jule," he barks in the direction of the kitchen, "come here and dispose of that wretched bird."

But before the slave girl can pass through the kitchen door, his daughter stops her, touching a hand to her upturned arm. In this position the colors of their skin are nearly indistinguishable.

"Did you hear me, Jule?" says the father, old Frederick Dent. "Are you bringing my tray? Will you dispose of that bird at last? I swear, it's put me off my appetite."

"Yes, sir," says Jule, with a desperate glance at the hand that blocks her without exerting even the slightest pressure. The intent alone is enough.

"Jule has her hands full," says his daughter. "I'll see to Birdie myself."

"I require no excuses for that girl's shortcomings. Especially from you." The old planter—known in these precincts as "the colonel," although he has never served in any army known to God or man—coughs around the stem of his pipe. "*Birdie*," he mutters into his mustache, giving his head a little shake, as if the poor lump of feathers and flesh does not even deserve a name. It won't make a meal, so it had best be disposed of before it draws vermin.

He shakes his head again. *Birdie.* Ridiculous.

The colonel is no native to these parts. He comes from Maryland, where as a young man he found employment in the fur trade and forged a deep and unexamined sympathy with the Southern cause. White Haven is the name he gave this rich tract of Missouri farmland, and a white haven it is. Its acres yield up wheat by the bushel and corn by the wagonload along with every fruit known to grow upon twig or vine or bush. Its population of chickens and sheep and milk cows is constantly in flux and thus without accurate number. The Gravois Creek runs sparkling through its heart, teeming with fish. To maintain this Eden requires the ceaseless toil of thirty-six black slaves, to say nothing of the colonel's occasional contributions in the way of general oversight.

The daughter and the slave girl are nearly the same age, and by coincidence they are both named Julia. The black girl goes by "Jule," the last two syllables of her Christian name having been lopped off in the service of clarity. She makes now for the head of the table where the colonel waits, his lower lip jutting and his round belly keeping him a few inches farther from his plate than is entirely convenient. He puts down his pipe and harrumphs in her direction as she draws near, and then he harrumphs once more toward Julia as she approaches the sideboard. Jule takes up the colonel's empty soup plate and replaces it with his entrée—fried chicken, biscuits with gravy, quivering slices of some kind of aspic—while Julia takes up the linen bed holding Birdie and squares it bravely at the level of her heart.

"So when did the creature expire?"

"Shortly after dawn. Suddenly."

"We should expect no miracles from it, I suppose."

"Father?"

"No resurrection, I mean. After three days of mourning."

"Father, I shall miss him and I shall miss his song."

"The trees are full of birds," says the colonel, taking up a drumstick. He dismisses her with a wave of its greasy stob. "Now away with that one, before you spoil my digestion entirely."

Julia wonders if the young lieutenant will visit today. She knows that she has no right to make even so light a claim upon him, no right in all the world, but she wonders all the same. Her mind does the knowing and her heart does the wondering and there is no clear way to reconcile the two.

She steps out onto the porch and takes a seat on the swing. Its chain creaks under her weight but then it always creaks, even in the littlest breeze. The sound of it is a constant around here, like work. She places the bird beside her and idly caresses his little round head with one finger. In life, Birdie had no patience for such treatment. That she can accomplish it now is a broken dream come true, and it draws a tear to her eye.

She dabs away the tear with the back of her hand, wondering again or perhaps still if the young lieutenant might be planning to visit today. He could be on his way even now. Anything is possible. He first came to White Haven at the invitation of her older brother, Fred, his roommate at West Point. Fred thought the world of the lieutenant and said so by way of introduction, and Julia has thus far found no reason to differ. In recent months the lieutenant's appearances have become increasingly frequent—two or even three times a week, whether her brother is on the premises or not, he will ride the five miles from Jefferson Barracks so as to pass a pleasant hour or two—and although he always pays his respects to the colonel, she is becoming quite certain that visiting with him is not his only aim. Far from it. The truth is, he enters her father's presence with the sturdy gloom of a man going into battle, and he takes his leave like a prisoner set free.

She dares not think that he might be coming on her account. She dares not think it, and yet think it she does. She thinks it and she desires it and she wishes it with all her bereft and birdless heart, squeezing her eyes shut and gritting her teeth and sending that message out into the ether as if the lieutenant might possess some mystical receptor that would let him detect it and interpret it and, based upon its urgency, stir himself to the heroic action of her rescue.

It takes him until the middle of the afternoon. She is upstairs, looking out her bedroom window, the bird wrapped in its white linen and lying on the sill. He arrives without ceremony astride an anonymous army horse that seems to know her way and to be in no special hurry, judging by how she idles along the farm lane, nosing at the bits of grass that sprout up around the fence posts. She turns in at the gate and makes for the wooden trough alongside the barn, and her rider permits her. He sits the horse while she drinks her fill and then he dismounts and ties her up loosely and proceeds to the house. Everyone knows him and he greets them all one after another, hired man and slave alike. He glances at one point toward her window but she cannot tell if he sees her or only the reflected world. The look upon his face in that instant—in half shadow beneath the brim of his hat—is impossible to read.

"Lieutenant Grant," cries Jule from the foyer at his knock, and upstairs Julia hears the words with the very soles of her feet.

His old roommate's little sister. If there could be a plainer and less romantic connection than this, she cannot imagine it. She sits on the end of the bed and looks out the window, chewing her lip and bemoaning her fate. *His old roommate's little sister.* It is a poor place to start. Yet he has come once again, has he not? He can be no more than twenty or thirty feet away at this very instant, dutifully and deferentially making small talk in the sweltering oven of her father's dim, hot, airless office. She ought to rejoice in his nearness and in the promise of his calling on her once the colonel is finished with him. She ought to rejoice in this as she rejoices in so many aspects of the charmed life she leads. She is a most fortunate girl, after all—in good health, adored by her family, and secure in the sheltered and bountiful world of White Haven. She should appreciate the gifts she has been given, and not go seeking trouble. She settles her mind on this idea and she lets her gaze drift—from the fields to the barnyard and from the barnyard to the walk and from the walk to her own windowsill, whereon lies the bird. *Yes.* It is Birdie's death that has her in this wounded mood. That's all there is to it.

She slips from the bed and puts her ear to the floorboards and can nearly make out the words that filter up from below as her father regales the lieutenant with one of his disquisitions. An occasional grunt of agreement from his young visitor serves as a kind of punctuation, but otherwise it is a solo performance. If she has learned anything in her eighteen years, it's that once her father gets started, there is rarely need or opportunity for anyone else to put in a word. The colonel possesses refined and unshakable opinions on most everything created by God during His six days of labor, as well as a list of things He ought to have undertaken on that first misspent Sabbath.

At least, she thinks, *He managed to create Lieutenant Ulysses S. Grant.*

Time passes and the shadows in the barnyard begin to lengthen and the conversation from the room below, if conversation it may be called, slows and stalls and sputters to a halt. She knows from previous visits that the lieutenant shall be released at any moment, and since there are few other family members around for him to call upon today, she must head downstairs directly if their paths are to cross before he takes his leave. She very nearly brings the bird to show him but thinks better of it at the last moment, for as much as she desires the lieutenant to comfort her, she desires even more for her father to believe that she has obeyed him and disposed of the body. So she takes the empty cage down from its hook and carries that instead. She times her steps that she might meet the lieutenant in the front hall or the little sitting room or perhaps the dim parlor beyond it as he exits her father's office. Surely enough, her strategy works.

"Julia!" he calls from the shadows. "Are you taking your friend out for some fresh air?"

She stops, lifts the cage that he may see it more clearly from where he stands, and gives him a look composed of knitted eyebrows and woe.

"My goodness," says the lieutenant. "He's flown the coop!"

"Worse," says Julia.

"Worse?"

"He's passed."

"No." He rushes to her side.

"Yes."

"When?"

"Just this morning."

He takes the cage from her, and although it weighs nothing it is as if he is lifting a considerable burden.

"Lieutenant Grant . . ."

"Ulysses. Please."

"Ulysses."

He gives the empty cage an appraising look. "What has become of the body?"

"Upstairs." She sniffs a little. "In my room."

He studies her face. Her eyes are clear and her cheeks are pale and there is no particular sign that she has been crying, yet the overall impression that she gives is one of weariness and grief. He gives her a kindly smile and indicates the way upstairs with a tilt of his head. "Perhaps you could fetch him. We ought to be attending to the obsequies."

She leaves him holding the cage and dashes up the stairs, her expression just a shade or two brighter than she would desire it to be in a world any less perfect than this.

He asks her to wait a bit while he takes the cage to the barn and sees about one thing or another. In the yard he finds the black stable boy and inquires as to the availability of a saw and a hammer and some little nails. Also a scrap or two of lumber. The boy advises him that although the man who does carpentry has gone to town and left his toolshed locked up, he knows where the key is hidden. His manner suggests that he knows the plantation's every last secret, not just this one, and Grant suspects that he might. Children, regardless of their color, always know secrets.

The boy leads him around behind the toolshed but has second thoughts at the last moment. Is Grant to be trusted? There could be grave consequences otherwise. The lieutenant assures him that he will leave everything—including their secret—intact and in good order. The boy, satisfied or at least placated, scrambles around to the back of the shed and prizes away a loose board to reveal the key.

There is lumber inside the shed, white pine by the look of it, sawn thin and cut for clapboards. Its grain is straight and its lengths are without bending or warpage. He shall need only a bit. He measures out his work and scribes a few lines and saws the pieces off clean, and then he fits them together by hand as a trial. He frowns in satisfaction and makes adjustments here and there with a plane, a file, a sanding block. It takes no time at all. He goes on to prepare a flat lid for the box with a shallow rim around its edge, fitting closely but not too close. A less thoughtful individual might have resolved simply to nail the top on once the bird had been gotten inside, but that would never do.

A little jar of yellow paint on a high dim shelf catches his eye, its spilled traces glowing like the yolk of an egg. The contents prove nearly dried-up, but a splash of turpentine remedies that. He finds a scrap of wood to stir it and it yields up a thin mixture that gives the wood a faint yellow sheen more than paints it. But it dries rapidly, which is in its favor. He leaves the box and the lid to finish drying on a crate just inside the barn door and he sends the boy to fetch him back a spade, along with a Holy Bible if he can find one.

He seems to recall that the book of Matthew has something to say about birds, but when he finds the text it proves to be anything but complimentary as to their value. He chooses a psalm instead. "I will lift up mine eyes unto the hills, from whence cometh my help." He has heard that one read at a funeral or two, and he will live to hear it read at many more.

The boy assumes that he is to be charged with digging the grave, but Grant releases him to go about his business. He and Julia choose a sunny spot in the flower garden, just at the foot of a trellis that supports an ancient climbing rose, and he digs the hole. In the shade of the porch they arrange the body in its little yellow coffin and close the lid.

"Tell me, Ulysses," she says as she stands before the climbing rose, the box in her hands. "Are you merely humoring me?"

"Never."

"I mean, Father says . . ."

He touches her wrist. "What does your heart say?"

"Oh, Ulysses."

"This is not for your father, Julia. It's not even for Birdie, or not entirely. It's for you." He kneels and takes the box and sets it into the grave and covers it. The mound is hardly larger than his hand. The bird is gone and yet it shall be here forever. A yellow bird in a yellow box beneath a red, red rose.

He straightens up and rubs the dirt from his hands with a kerchief, and then he finds the psalm and reads it aloud. He does not linger over any of it, and when he is finished he closes the Bible like any utilitarian thing that has served its purpose. Like the spade, like the box, like his muddied handkerchief. He glances up when he is done and through the front window he makes out the silhouette of the colonel himself, paused and watching. He waits an instant in a kind of silent defiance before he looks away for good.

Forty Days and Forty Nights

Transporting him to the Adirondacks required a modified railroad car on loan from William Vanderbilt, conveying him up the heights of Mount McGregor required a private narrow-gauge train, and getting him up the path to the borrowed cottage required two men straining at the handles of an oversized three-wheeled perambulator. The apparatus, intended for seaside use by the invalid class, seems as out of place at this mountain retreat as the general feels when he must travel in it. Gone are the days when he could sit a horse, any horse, broken or unbroken, the wilder and more ill-tempered, the better.

No one knows how much time remains to him upon this earth, but the hope is that some fresh Adirondack air will buy a few additional weeks. Perhaps more. At this extremity—after a year of battling the illness that has brought him to this final outpost, a year of toiling desperately on his infernal memoirs to the exclusion of almost everything else—the margins are thin.

In the end, he shall be granted slightly more than a month. Not quite forty days and not quite forty nights, but near enough to that ancient measure of the unendurable.

The rolling perambulator stands empty on the porch just now, and the sublime mountain views that grace the cottage go largely unappreciated. He is toiling away indoors. He is conjuring. He is dreaming. He is bringing the dead, and the dead past, back to life.

His mind plays its dependable tricks of retrieval and restoration, and scenes from the war appear as if he is not just recalling them but witnessing them for the very first time. He gets almost nothing wrong, at least nothing of significance. As diligently as his son Fred searches the printed records and compares story against story, he can find few contradictions.

Dr. Douglas has taken a room at the Hotel Balmoral—luxurious, brand-new, and just up the walking path from the cottage—so as to be available around the clock. Toward the end he will rarely stray from his patient's side. He is Grant's contemporary and has known him for ages, although these days no one doubts that his patient will predecease him by a wide margin. Their paths first crossed at Shiloh, when the doctor was working for the Sanitary Commission. Grant plotted the destruction of the Confederates, while Douglas oversaw the delivery of medical treatment to the Union armies. Every soldier that took a ball or a blade under the general's aegis received a bed or a dose of Soldier's Joy at the direction of the doctor.

During the early days at Mount McGregor, the general often mutters to himself as he works. He has not lost his voice entirely, although it will slip away in time. For now, it burbles and hitches its way up from the clotted depths of his throat as he huddles in his chair, papers on a lap desk and a pencil in his hand. He is concealed beneath blankets heaped up around his neck, sufficiently invisible that an unwary visitor might think these ragged moans and mutterings an aspect of some daylight haunting. Perhaps he is trying out sentences before committing them to the page. Perhaps he is repeating things that he hears his old compatriots saying from times long ago.

Sherman in the field, dust covered and bleeding.

Lincoln in a cabin on a high bluff in Virginia.

A nameless soldier in a moonlit wood, even nearer to death than the general is now.

The present has grown slippery, but the past holds still. This suits him fine. The past is all that he needs now. As long as he retains his memories, he shall have a fair chance of completing his work.

As to the malleability of the present, this one example. He has just now heard the mantel clock strike eleven, although its hands point to twelve and his trusty pocket watch shows noon as well. He complains about it to Fred, his oldest son and lately his factotum, who sits at the table opposite.

"Fix the clock," he says in his voice of dust. "It struck only eleven." Before long, after his speech has failed, communicating seven such words will seem to him a tragic waste—for in taking the time and strength to write them out on paper, he would be trading away a different seven that would not find their way into the day's writing. A man, even this man, can do only so much. It is the unpitying calculus of decline.

Fred nods and goes to the mantelpiece and leans in to fuss with the clock, as if doing so might make the slightest difference. He is only humoring his father. He heard it strike twelve, as plain as day. Where his father's consciousness may have gone during the unwitnessed stroke is a mystery. The old general—and a general he is again, restored after so many years to the rank that he gave up to serve as president (not only the rank but the pension that went with it, both honors recovered at this late date when even the striking of the clock has become unreliable)—shows no particular sign of having drifted away. But Fred can feel it in his bones. He has felt it before. His father was elsewhere. Thank God he has come back.

Soon enough—a week, a month, says the doctor—he will be lost and gone forever.

He has just now lived through Chattanooga again. He dares to hope that when every fact from those terrible days is finally set down on paper, they will all fade from his mind—that as the waning months of the war unspool onto the page, he will grow increasingly unburdened by memory. He will be left to drift through his last days with the lightly furnished mind of a child.

Until then, he must toil away. He is obliged to history. He is obliged to the men who fought beneath him. He is obliged to Clemens. And he is obliged above all to Julia and the children. He cannot let them go impoverished into their long days on account of his mistakes. When he is gone from this earth, there will be no more charitable fundraising to offset his debts. There will be no more anonymous bank drafts slipped under the door. There will be no more benefactors housing the lot of them for nothing in a sumptuous mountain cottage like this.

All of that kindness will die with him, and soon enough. It is his duty to make things right before that day arrives and the opportunity for setting the world straight has passed forever.

CHAPTER 2

1856

Hardscrabble

"Who ain't a slave? Tell me that."

The hired man's name is Elwood Marshall, and he lives on an adjacent property gone to ruin under his attentions, and he is every bit as accomplished a philosopher as he is a farmer. He is missing three teeth that show and two that don't and one finger that he has learned to manage without. Old Colonel Dent despises him for a rustic.

Aside from Marshall and Grant, the men working this stubborn and plaguey ground are slaves indeed, slaves for certain, slaves on loan from White Haven that they may enjoy the pleasure of breaking their backs in the service of Dent's daughter. Elwood Marshall is the only man present who will profit a single dollar from the day's toil.

Nonetheless, he goes on. "Those boys get bed and board, guaranteed," he says. "What do I get?"

"You get a day's pay for a day's work," says Grant.

"A day's pay don't even last a day." Marshall puts down his shovel and indicates the black men. "A fellow minds his manners in *their* line of work," he says, "and he's fixed for life."

"Then I'd recommend giving their line of work a try."

"Don't tempt me. I like things steady."

"You own a farm, Elwood. That's steady."

"A farm's a drain on a man. You'll see that, you live long enough."

Ulysses has already seen. For two years now, ever since he quit the army, he has worked to improve this property. He built the house with his own hands, aided by a pair of slaves belonging to Dent. They downed the trees and they dug the cellar and they set the foundations. They shaved the timbers and they put up the walls and they shingled the roof. It is a homely log cabin, two rooms up and two down, with space for a pigsty and a kitchen garden. The entire property is nothing but space, come to that, nothing but space stretching for eighty acres all around. Some of it will be planted in wheat and some in potatoes. Some of it will stay woodlot and some will be apple orchard.

He and Julia call the place by its truest possible name: Hardscrabble.

The slaves who aided in this feat of creation, and who work Hardscrabble still, are known as John and Daniel. They are brothers to Jule, whose duties now are to look after Grant's wife and children. The slave woman is pleasant and capable in the extreme, if from time to time a trifle insolent. Grant does not begrudge her this eccentricity, for she has earned it by long and close service. Jule has been Julia's companion since youth, after all, and Julia finds humor in her occasional impertinence.

These eighty acres were a wedding gift from the colonel, as is the labor of these slaves, but like most gifts they are not without attachments. No sooner does Ulysses begin to get on his feet than he is burdened with managing Dent's White Haven in addition to his own property. He is overseer and livestock manager and chief agronomist.

He balances the books and he mends the fences and he shoots the occasional fox that finds its way into the henhouse. The hired hands and the enslaved blacks witness the scope of his engagement, and while they may respect it, Dent does not. He will never draw from Ulysses enough work to balance the loss of his daughter.

Two years in Missouri have earned Grant an acquaintance with slavery, but they have failed to give him any comfortableness with it. To Julia's family the institution is as homely and necessary as rain, but to a young man raised in Ohio according to his father's abolitionist principles, it is a puzzle at best and an error in management at worst. White Haven and Hardscrabble could be run other ways—ordinary ways—with little loss of profit.

He resolves that when his acreage is tamed and his fortune is secured, he shall return John and Daniel to his father-in-law and hire some free men of his own. White or black, it will make no difference. Work is work and pay is pay. He will send Elwood Marshall packing as well, for the man is more trouble than the most recalcitrant slave. For now, to keep peace within the family, he will bear the shackles of this peculiar institution without complaint.

Autumn is coming on and the earth is beginning to lock down. As the day begins to fold in upon itself, he eyes the low sun and checks his pocket watch. Satisfied that he has an hour's time before supper, he leaves the others to finish their work and hitches the old horse to the hay wagon and rattles off to make up a load of wood. He has a shed full of it stacked for his own use behind the house right now—enough to last the season, if the cabin is as tight as he believes he has made it. The wood that he will load up today will be for sale. He has cobbled together a little shelter in the southernmost woodlot, a roof without sides half-hung among the trees like some dire forest spirit, and under the protection of it he keeps logs laid up to dry. Cutting it to stove length and splitting it and stacking it is labor that seems to him like recreation in some ways, for it takes place on no particular schedule and with no demand beyond what he can get for it on the streets of St. Louis. He cuts it when he can and he sells it when he must. The money carries weight, for these old trees are nearly all of the bounty that this land has yet yielded up. He is glad to have them.

He draws a canvas over the wagonload of wood and ties it down for the return home. He has a word with Marshall regarding the work to be addressed tomorrow, and he sends the slaves back to White Haven under the hired man's supervision. But Marshall is not ready to go, not quite. Something has come up, he says, and he requires an advance on his pay if it would not be too much trouble. Although the thing that has come up probably involves whiskey, it is no business of Grant's to ask. His pocket is as empty as the next man's, as empty as always, but from a lockbox beneath his desk he scrapes together just enough to suit the hired man's needs.

He stands on the front step and watches the men go off down the lane until they vanish into a declivity. A cold breeze gusts in from the north. He steps inside and latches the door against the chill of it and presses the flat of his palm to the wall, hoping for the best. In the morning he shall take the wagon to St. Louis.

Peddling firewood by the armload is no path to great wealth. In the warm months he has few customers and they are generally as poor as he is, scrabbling city folks burdened with rent to pay and mouths to feed and a kitchen stove to keep charged no matter how hot the weather and how stifling their rooms. They pay to burn firewood when they can't scavenge sufficient trash. Wood from his lot is in no way superior to the leg of a cast-off table fallen from the junkman's wagon, or to the mullions of a window frame lying broken in an alley. Wood from a woodlot can be the poorer choice, in fact, because sifting through its ashes will never yield up a nail that might be hammered straight for a second use.

He would give these people his firewood if he could. From time to time he does.

The approach of colder weather brings out those with better resources, preparing in advance for hard days to come. Last night's cold snap seems to have struck them as a signal, for they are out in force and his wagon is empty not long after ten o'clock by his watch. All told, the contents of the cashbox will fit in his pocket, and not because the bills are large. Very little of it is in fact folding money. He tethers the old horse to a hitching post and goes for a little walk around the town, which is crowded and boisterous. The doors of druggists and jewelers and general stores are thrown open to the last of the good weather. These busy people with their preparedness and their commitment to commerce get him thinking about the winter ahead as he ambles from storefront to storefront, his clothes streaked with sawdust and pine sap, a farmer in the big town with a little money jingling in his pocket.

In one window he spies a flannel nightgown that would suit Julia to perfection. He enters the shop to consider it and finds on the shelves further nightshirts in sizes to suit the children, Fred and Nellie and Buck. He wipes his hand on his trousers and tries the fabric between thumb and forefinger. How soft it is. How warm it would be on a cold winter's night. How sweetly his wife and children would sleep.

He tallies up the cost, and his hope falters. He jingles the coins in his pocket and draws them out and counts them up again without any improvement. He frowns, calculates, frowns again. Perhaps, if he is careful and lucky and above all industrious, he could put aside enough money by Christmas. He finds the clerk and puts down the minimum required to have the garments laid by, and then he quits dallying and goes out to drive the old horse back to the farm. For a good while now he has had his eye on a couple of deadfalls weathering at the edge of a high pasture, and he reckons they may have seasoned long enough by now. Today would be an excellent day to find out.

Having arranged for Ulysses to oversee the farm, Colonel Dent now has more time to indulge his critical faculties. Nothing upon which his eye falls—the part in a man's hair, the rhythm of a horse's gait, the quantity of ice in a snifter of rye, the wag of a dog's tail, the tinder expended to light a fire, the crust on a biscuit, the pepper in his gravy—nothing is entirely satisfactory. He is a Niagara of complaint.

His son-in-law wonders why a man who knows the best way to do everything has gone so long without putting a single thing right on his own property. Why he has never repaired a shutter or swept out a hen-house. Why he has not so much as straightened a curtain. Perhaps the gap between knowing what is correct and bothering to do it has driven him mad.

His complaint today has to do with a slave, and he brings it to his son-in-law at second or third hand. He has obtained it from the hired man, Marshall. Marshall has it on good authority that the man in question, an old slave named Clark, has been pilfering firewood and passing it along to a young slave woman on the next farm over. A person might think he was courting her this way if courting were the word for it and if Clark were not a million years of age. The quantities of wood are no doubt modest, only as much as a fellow might conceal in a pant leg, but regardless of that and regardless of Clark's carnal intentions, the resources of White Haven are being sapped—worse than sapped: they are being effectively transferred to the fellow who runs the adjoining farm, a young German with a fine purebred riding horse and a haughty manner—without Colonel Dent's approval or even his knowledge, at least until now.

"That's an interesting story," says Grant. "How do you suppose Marshall has come by it?"

"The men in Clark's cabin report a shortage."

"They complain to Marshall?"

"They complain to someone, I suppose. Someone who passes it along."

"I see."

"Marshall keeps his ear to the ground."

Grant laughs. "He ought to be keeping his nose to the grindstone."

"Be that as it may," says Dent, "the pilferage goes on unchecked. I am being taken advantage of and no doubt mocked behind my back. It is disloyalty to a criminal degree. You must see to it."

See to it he does. He waits until after supper. The moon is bald and lonesome in the night sky and he saddles up the old horse and rides to where the slave quarters huddle on the windy edge of White Haven. The fence line marking the adjoining property—the farm where the woman is purported to live—is not much distant, and he can see how a man could carry a little firewood out to it from time to time.

He knocks on a door so shrunken in its frame that it might as well be open. A man comes to admit him, and when he steps inside he finds six more bent around a little iron stove. They startle at the sight of him and strain to stand up in weary obeisance. The room ought to house four and wouldn't house any if there were kindness remaining in the world. A

21

couple of broken bedsteads and a mattress of rope burned in places and the rest of the furnishings just straw pallets on the floor. Wind whistling in through a hundred cracks and knotholes. He thinks of his own cabin, of its rough-hewn logs and its raw chinking imperfectly done, and by comparison it seems a palace.

But this hovel belongs to Dent, not to him. What goes on here is Dent's business.

The dim red light in the shack comes filtered by ashes, but there is enough of it that he can identify Clark. He signals to him and they withdraw to the doorway and step outside. The other men watch them go and murmur to one another in a satisfied way. Misery loves company, but everything has limits. Another man's troubles may provide at least a distraction from your own.

"Sir?"

Grant indicates the fence line and the farm beyond it. "You know anything about Keller's place? That German?"

"Not too much, sir."

"Is he good to his people?"

"I couldn't say, sir."

"Know anybody lives there?"

"Yes, sir. I do." He brightens a little. Even in the blowing winter moonlight Grant can see it.

"Friend of yours?"

"Family, sir. She's my sister's child."

"Is that a fact. Where's your sister?"

"In the grave a long time ago. Down in Mississippi."

"How'd the daughter end up here?"

Clark gives a shrug. "I ain't heard about it till last month."

"She doing all right?"

22

"Thank you kindly for asking. I expect she suffers some in this cold weather, coming up from Mississippi and all."

Grant considers. The wind picks up and he shifts a few degrees to shield Clark from it. "You know that woodlot of mine?"

"Yes."

"The one down toward the south end?"

"I know it."

"There's plenty down there. If the supply here runs low, I want you to make up the shortfall."

"Sir?"

"You personally. Take another man, take a wheelbarrow, take a mule and a wagon if you need to. Bring back what you can use."

"What about Colonel Dent?"

"It's my woodlot, not his."

"I see."

"I want every soul supplied. Friend and family alike. No one should suffer in this cold."

"Yes, sir."

"Do you understand me, Clark?"

"I understand, sir."

"Entirely?"

"Yes, sir."

"All right. Make sure you take from what I haven't already split. You can split it yourself."

"I can."

"Good."

"Thank you, sir."

"Go on back inside now."

"I will, sir."

Grant mounts the horse and returns home. Julia has put the children to bed and caught up on some mending and finally gone to bed herself. He douses the lamp and climbs under the quilts, but it is forever before he can get warm.

In the morning he rides once more to White Haven. He finds the colonel not behind his desk but partaking of a leisurely breakfast, and although the old man frowns at the interruption, Grant draws a cup of coffee from the urn and takes a seat opposite him. He wastes no time getting started.

"If there's been any wrongdoing as to Clark," he says, "it was ours."

The colonel looks stricken. "*Ours?*"

"Ours. We've shorted those men the necessities."

"*We?*" says the colonel, and Grant catches his meaning. They are his men and his burden, and as long as he is above the sod, no son-in-law will begin claiming even their troubles for his own.

"Fine," he says. "*You've* shorted them, then. Those devils are freezing to death."

"They have shelter. They have clothing. They have provisions."

"Only the minimum. A weak man can do little work, Colonel. A dead man can do none. And an unhappy man may accomplish more harm than good."

"Such a man will be punished. Leather and iron, that's the answer. Leather and iron."

Grant narrows his eyes. "Does a wise man abuse his possessions, or does he look after them?"

"I care for those creatures like family, and they know it."

"Families look after their own, Colonel. Clark does."

"Tell me, exactly what has that black bastard done?"

"Nothing of any account. And as reward for his good faith, I have named him quartermaster of the woodpile."

"Meaning?"

"He is in charge of dispensing its contents."

The colonel scoffs. "The usual way of handling firewood has always worked perfectly well. My supplies are not without limit."

"Damn your supplies. I told him to use mine."

Dent scoffs. "There'll be no end to his thievery."

"He'll take what's needed."

"He'll impoverish you, mark my word."

Grant shifts his weight.

"You lack experience with these individuals. You don't know them."

Grant sets down his cup and pushes back his chair. "I know that a man ought to care for his belongings," he says. "I know need when I see it. And I know that a black skin may cover a true heart as well as a white one."

Clark and the rest take no advantage as the winter goes along, but their needs are appreciable. Grant watches the woodpile as it dwindles, gauging its shrinkage against the passage of time. He watches the weather and the calendar. Market days come and often enough he chooses to stay home rather than add to the ongoing depletion. The people of St. Louis will have to do without his supply this year, and so be it. They possess alternatives that the men and women in those shacks do not.

If he is careful, and if a cold spell does not set in during January, they shall all survive until the springtime unscathed.

Christmas draws near, and the funds in his cashbox are short. He could afford the nightgown for Julia or the three nightshirts for the children, but not the entire lot. He blames himself. The problem originated with his father-in-law, and the hardship fell upon the backs of the powerless slaves, but the plan for resolving it was his entirely. There is only so much good to go around in the world. Suffering shall always be plentiful, but relief is limited and must be parceled out with care.

He rides to the city on the day before Christmas. He goes without the wagon and without a stick of wood. He goes without so much as a single coin in his pocket. He ties up the horse and enters the jewelry store beneath a bell that chimes to announce his arrival. Intensive negotiations ensue, at the conclusion of which the jeweler takes his watch in exchange for twenty-two dollars. Not a penny more.

What use, after all, does a farmer have for a watch? His work requires no more precision in the matter of time than a calendar can provide— and if a calendar is not at hand, he can make do with the moon and stars. The work is ancient, and it runs on an ancient cycle.

He enters the general mercantile and pays his balance, along with a little extra to have the garments wrapped. Then, with the packages secured in his saddlebags, he rides home beneath a light sifting of snow, perfectly content.

CHAPTER 3

1862

The Cigar

He has been a pipe smoker when he has smoked at all, for he finds something meditative in it. A man cannot smoke a pipe while he is otherwise occupied. It requires concentration and a steady hand. It requires commitment. A pipe—any pipe, from the lowliest corncob to the loftiest meerschaum—must be loaded with all the care a fellow would apply to the charging of field artillery. Once lit, it must be tended and nursed and encouraged like a green battalion. And when the tobacco is burned out at last and all of the pleasure has been extracted from it, the pipe smoker is still not finished. His implement must be cooled, cleaned, and dried thoroughly. Like an army, it must have its rest.

The cigar in question, then, is just a moment's dalliance. A battlefield convenience made possible by the insistent generosity of a certain naval officer, one Andrew Foote, just before the assault on Fort Donelson. He presses it upon Grant as they part company, and Grant finds it in his pocket a while later, and in the heat of the battle he puts a light to it. In keeping with the ease and transparency of smoking a cigar—it requires nothing of a man but respiration—he then proceeds to forget about it entirely. He draws upon it no more than a dozen times altogether and relights it as required. It remains either in his hand or between his teeth for the duration of the battle, even after it has expired.

Its persistence draws attention. Its persistence and its ubiquity, for Grant is everywhere that day and he carries his cigar with him. Afoot or on horseback, freezing on the field or huddled by the fire at headquarters, scouting from a high ridge or kneeling to divine the Rebel strategy from the contents of a prisoner's knapsack, he is as omnipresent as some warlike god. Hardly a man on either side fails to catch a glimpse of him and the smoldering talisman he bears.

The newspapermen notice it as well, and the cigar finds its way into their accounts. If Grant is the venerated hero of the day, that stubborn cigar lends him a reassuring touch of plain humanity. His reputation—indeed, his personal mythology—grows by the hour whether he likes it or not, but the cigar keeps him a trifle ordinary. It shows him to be a man you might mend a fence with.

The first packages arrive even before he decamps from Nashville. They appear at his desk like eager volunteers, compliments of admirers that include a medical doctor from Chicago, a shopkeeper from Pittsburgh, and an anonymous band of Unionist tobacco growers located somewhere in Virginia. Chicago sent twenty-five cheroots in a carton, Pittsburgh sent a dozen robustos in a handmade crate done up with his likeness burned into the lid, and Virginia sent an uncountable quantity varying in shape and size and wrapped in crisp white paper, tied with a ribbon of Union blue.

He distributes these riches to his officers and men with the open hand of a new father, in the process making himself a greater hero than ever. A handful he retains, and he applies himself to them one after another as he attends to the day's correspondence. The man who nursed one cigar for the entire assault on Fort Donelson goes through a half dozen before nightfall.

The next day there are more. A dozen packages and then some, two or three hundred cigars altogether. On the third day, when he finally sets out for Washington, he must leave behind a mountain of them. Carrying so many would require a separate wagon, and shipping them would be a terrible waste of resources. He leaves instructions that any letters accompanying further such gifts should be forwarded that he may reply, but the cigars themselves should go to the men. They have earned them.

More cigars prove to be waiting in Washington, cigars by the pallet and by the bale and by the hogshead, with no army to help him use them up. He commits himself to smoking them in earnest now, keeping at it from morning till night, and he decides that while they require very little fuss and attention, which suits them to his peripatetic way of life, they are nearly as conducive to rumination as a well-maintained pipe. Thus is he converted. Over the coming weeks, boxes of the seductive things will follow his movements around the countryside like iron filings in pursuit of a magnet. He will have all the cigars a man could ever require. Eventually he shall go through twenty-five of them every day of the week.

They will kill him in time. But for now they are a kindness and a comfort.

Forty Days and Forty Nights

The family that has gathered in this mountainside cottage—Julia, of course, and Fred and Buck and Jesse and their wives, and Nellie, dear Nellie, home from England—have learned not just to take his pulse but to assess the rhythm of his heart by means of a stethoscope that hangs from a peg near his chair. They prod him in the most familiar of ways, hoping to save Dr. Douglas from being awakened in the hotel and having to dash down the trail to the cottage. Thus far they have been successful. The patriarch endures it all in good spirits, and he might nearly enjoy it if he would permit himself. The touch of these beloved hands upon his ailing body.

So far there has been just one very close thing. It comes late in the evening, when the doctor has gone off to his quarters and Julia has taken herself to bed and Nellie alone sits up with her father. Predictable dark arrived at ten o'clock, when a caretaker shut down the generator at the Hotel Balmoral and the electricity winked out and the past once more established its dominion over the mountain.

The general sighs and scribbles away by the light of a candle on a side table. The night is balmy and the windows are open and every time some trickster breeze sweeps toward him past the flame a little

31

smoke will catch in his throat and he will be taken by a coughing fit. Under the hood of his blanket, by the yellow gleam of the candle, his ravaged face glows red. His daughter will fix him with a look both pitying and terrified as he strains for breath, but in a moment or two he recovers.

"Perhaps we should close the window, Father."

"No. Thank you."

"Or light an oil lamp instead."

"No. The candlelight suits me. It restores me to a certain time and place."

And so they go on, the father transferring the past to the page, the daughter holding her own breath and listening to his. The clock on the mantelpiece chimes some hour that will never come again.

Another gust of wind, and one more hitch in his breathing. One more pinpoint of soot caught in his treasonous throat. This time he cannot seem to clear it. He coughs into his fist, throws off the blankets, and clutches at his swollen neck. Nellie comes around behind the chair and pounds upon his back, to no avail. Perhaps she goes easy, for unwrapped from his heavy blankets he seems to her no more substantial than a songbird. Perhaps it is futile. Regardless, the action yields little improvement.

"Mr. Terrell!" she calls at last. "Come! Mr. Terrell!" Her parents and her brothers call him by his first name—Harrison—but Nellie, accustomed to formal dealings with a certain Mr. Wilkinson, her butler in England, grants him the honorific.

Terrell sleeps in a pantry just off the dining room so that he might be ready for such a moment as this. He emerges with a clattering of pots, his nightshirt askew and his feet bare, and dashes straight to the chair where the general sits pitched forward and straining for breath.

"We need Dr. Douglas," he says, but Nellie makes no response. She keeps her hand upon her father's shoulder even as Terrell lifts him from his seat for freer movement. He bends the general over his left arm and claps him between the shoulder blades. Nothing. "We need Douglas," he says, anguished, and he strikes the general on the back once more. He clears a space on the floor and lays him out flat and kneels beside him to begin breathing into his mouth, as he would for a drowning man. At the earliest opportunity, he tilts his head and gives Nellie a look so fierce and pleading that she unglues herself and takes off running up the mountain path.

When she returns with the doctor, her father is once again upright in his chair. He is terribly pale. His breathing is unsteady, and there is a little whistle in it that she cannot help but notice. Terrell reports that his pulse is elevated.

"And weak, I should think," says Douglas, kneeling alongside the general and bringing the stethoscope to his chest. "Oh, yes," he nods after a moment. "Very weak indeed, and most irregular."

Grant breathes, coughs, chokes, breathes again. He swallows with a wince.

"How is the pain?"

"Only a little worse than usual." He glances at his daughter as if realizing that he has betrayed some secret as yet unknown to her, when in truth she already knows everything.

"Allow me," says the doctor. He opens his bag and withdraws from it a stoppered vial of dilute cocaine. Terrell holds the candle high and Grant opens his mouth like a dutiful child and Douglas paints his throat with a saturated swab to dull the hurt. Grant chokes and Douglas lets him swallow and settle down for a moment before going at his throat again, this time with a freshly wetted swab and a long pair of tweezers. A moment's excavation yields up a marbled clot of mucus and blood and God knows what else, the removal of which eases the general's breathing a little. The doctor gives his throat one more lick of the medicine, then puts it away.

Grant dabs at his mouth with the back of his hand.

"Better?" asks the doctor.

Grant nods. "I shall be well enough to resume work."

"Perhaps not tonight," says Douglas. "Let's listen to your heart again." Its beating proves as ragged and weak as before, and Grant's overall aspect is little improved. The whistle is gone from his respiration, but the mere effort required to persist from moment to moment, to pass from present into present, seems to tax him dreadfully. Douglas reaches into his bag for a leather pouch stocked with syringes. He chooses one with a large barrel and fits a needle to it. "Fetch the brandy," he says to Terrell, "and I'll prepare a dose."

The first injection does little to restore him, so after thirty minutes' wait the doctor gives him a second. This time he adds a quantity of morphine to the alcohol, and this fortification seems to turn the tide. Grant's heartbeat strengthens and steadies, but his brain clouds. There shall be no more composition extracted from him tonight. Nellie settles him into his chair beneath his blankets. Douglas returns to the hotel and Terrell retakes his bed. The candle burns at a safe remove. Nellie goes to her room upstairs. The general dreams.

CHAPTER 4

1863

The Wrong Side of a Miracle

His leg pains him still. He cast aside his crutches weeks ago—abandoned the cursed things alongside the commode in the New Orleans hotel where he'd spent the summer recuperating—but over time the cane that he picked up instead has proven a poor substitute. Thus far, anyway. There is always tomorrow. He shall persevere.

If there was ever a good time to be suffering from a ruined hip—the painful product of spirited horseplay upon a spirited horse—these last few months have been just that. The action of the war has been in a kind of lull, a pause between Vicksburg and whatever horrors might come next. A man with a larger sense of his own importance might believe that the war has been biding its time on his account, waiting for the inconvenienced general to reengage before playing out its next act. But he knows otherwise. He knows that the war will go on with him or without him, on its own schedule and in its own time. War is always the master of a man, and not the reverse.

He is not in the field just now but at home with Julia and the children, stumping around on his bad leg and studying the trickle of reports that arrive daily from one front or another. The summer is wandering to a close and he is wandering with it, ill at ease and anxious. Chores around the place are relatively few, the entire business being set up to run without him while he is in Washington or posted on the battlefield.

Their wedding anniversary comes in August, and he and Julia mark it in ways that would have been impossible during their early impoverished years. He presents her with a locket holding painted likenesses of the children on one side and of himself on the other. Exactly when he has arranged to have these little portraits done she does not know. For her part, she has had made up the wedding ring that he has always gone without. It is a thin band of gold, as plain and unadorned as the two of them.

The trouble with his leg grows more tolerable and the thing that the war might bring next is suddenly imminent, so Grant makes up his mind to go and meet it halfway. He says his farewells to Julia and the children and he goes by steamboat from St. Louis to Cairo, and once in Cairo he boards a train for the two-day journey to Chattanooga. Everyone knows him but no one recognizes him, for he travels as always in his natural anonymous state. If he weren't a general he could be a spy, so unremarkable is his native condition.

For one thing, he is smaller than his reputation. Smaller and less ornamented and easier to miss. Slouched in his seat and barreling toward Nashville in the gathering twilight, he is clad as unprepossessingly as any rough-knuckled tradesmen. He wears cotton trousers of faded blue and a pale gray checked shirt minus a collar. His featureless blue overcoat is folded carefully and stowed on the seat to his right. His feet are posted squarely on the floorboards against the irregular rocking of the train, and upon them he wears black work boots, thorn-scarred and battered. Atop his head is a cap of white wool, knitted for him by Nellie as a Christmas present, drawn down close to his eyebrows.

He bears, in other words, no indication of his line of work, much less his rank. Only the grim set of his jaw might indicate that there is reason to pay him particular mind. The set of his jaw and the sparkle of his flashing eyes. Eyes as blue as the skies of his native Ohio, as blue as his lonesome traveling heart, as blue as the brightest hopes of the Union.

He awakens from a nightmare. A moonlit army is in panicked retreat, tumbling down a wooded ravine in massed and plummeting chaos, flags and the fallen crushed underfoot, bullets incoming from God knows what rifles set God knows where, men and horses dropping from prior wounds or falling wounded anew. Along the way they have set fire to wagons and armory carriages and precious stores, and their silhouettes leap up against the flames like devils. He cannot tell if the men are his or someone else's, and therefore he does not know whether he should encourage them with shouts or rout them with gunfire. What he does know—even here in this smoky and tumultuous dream—is that they are men, and they have lost something close to their hearts, and some of them are dying.

Shouts rouse him up. Shouts and a shuddering of the train as it slows.

He opens his eyes and straightens his back. As the train enters a long bend, he sees through the window a line of bonfires set like gemstones along the track. The sun has nearly set and the stars are coming out. The fires reflect in the glossy black sides of the passenger cars, doubling themselves again and again as the train flickers past. He sees men tending the fires, and he wonders what has brought them here. Where they have come from and what their intentions might be.

A porter comes through to light the lamps, and by the low bloom of their glow he catches sight of his ghost in the windowpane, white cap and wrinkled shirt and all. He snatches off the cap and rakes his fingers through his hair, making himself at least a shade more presentable. The act brings his face closer to the window, and the firelight illuminates his features from without, and a roar goes up from beyond the glass.

The men along the tracks are soldiers. He sees that now. Some are in uniform and some are in partial uniform and some are not in uniform at all, but they are soldiers every one. Union soldiers. His soldiers. They wave their hats and they shout his name and they bellow into the night like the hog callers that some of them would still be, were it not for this damned war.

Such cheering and hallooing you have never witnessed, for moments like this are reserved for very particular individuals. They are not meant for the common run. And whether you are the one being cheered or a member of the cheering throng, you will never forget it as long as you live. Eighty years into the future, men now barely past the age of consent will be telling stories of this night to their great-grandchildren. How word got out that General Grant would be on this train. How every available man came from all over Tennessee. How they not only saw the general with their own eyes but were actually seen by him in return.

Grant smiles down on them in spite of himself and they respond in kind, their upturned faces agleam in the light. Some of them snap to attention and offer a salute, which the general returns despite his dishevelment. To do less would be an act of disrespect. The train moves on and Grant draws his cheek up against the window and peers into the distance ahead.

By God, he thinks, *they've lighted the tracks all the way to Nashville.*

————

The Army of Mississippi has the bluecoats besieged at Chattanooga, determined to starve them out sooner or later. It is a slow and cruel path to victory but it has the advantages of being uncomplicated and more or less certain.

The boy—and a boy he is, having traded his short pants directly for these dusty butternut trousers—gazes down into the long valley and feels himself a conqueror. All he needs is patience. All that is required is that he follow orders, and his orders these last weeks have been something less than taxing. For the most part, the army is idle. The boy has brought along his violin from home and he plays it most of the time. The men called him "Fiddler Jim" at first, until his Christian name fell away from disuse. "Fiddler" he is now. The boy knows a handful of jigs and reels, a few waltzes and a hornpipe or two, and he goes through them all again and again both for practice and to pass the time. The men have tin ears and cannot tell one melody from another, so it makes no difference what he plays. At night they dance, one by one and two by two, their furious and ragged steps fueled by whiskey and firelight.

The boy wonders if the Union soldiers in the valley can hear his music. They might believe that it's being provided by some angel band as comfort in their time of peril. It could be so. He plays on, then, with his mind divided. He plays for the men capering around the fire and for the men starving to death in the valley. He hopes that this humane impulse does not make him a turncoat.

"Look at them fools dance," says a voice from over his shoulder. A boy older than he by two or three years. Just enough to make a difference. His name is Murphy, and he shares a tent with Jim and a few others, but as a rule he is too good to talk to most of them. Particularly a damned fiddle-playing kid. "You won't catch me dancing with another man," he says.

"Suit yourself," says Jim.

"You won't catch me dead."

"I heard you." He shrugs and plays on. "Then again, they got limited choices."

"I got limited choices too. I got the same limited choices, and you won't catch me dead."

"All right, then."

"Not with Sally waiting back home."

"Where's home again, anyway?"

"Rossville, Georgia."

Jim finishes his number and lowers his fiddle to fuss with a tuning peg that won't stay put. "You ain't far from there right now," he says. "Rossville."

"Shoot," says the older boy. "We in a whole different state. Shows how much you know."

"Your ass may be in Tennessee," says Jim, pointing due south with his bow. "But that right there? That's Georgia. Rossville ain't far."

"No."

"You could reach it with your rifle almost. Bury a bullet in Georgia dirt."

The older boy gawps into the starlit dark. "I never seen it from this direction."

"You never seen a lot."

"I just go where they tell me."

"I know."

"Keep my head down mostly."

"I know."

"You give me an idea, though."

He doesn't ask what that idea might be, since he believes he's already well ahead of Murphy in the way of ideas. Besides, the men around the fire have recovered their wind and are stamping their feet and hollering madly for another dance. Any tune will do—any tune at all.

For a man born in a prison cell, Braxton Bragg—commander of the Army of Mississippi—has risen a considerable distance. In the end it was not the conditions of his birth that proved the greatest burden but the difficulties that came afterward. The woes of a hapless child expelled from captivity into a world even less charitable. In time his mother would be cleared of the charge of murder, but the stain of it would linger and haunt the two of them forever. It lurks now in his long sad equine face and in his burning eyes and in the furious knot of his tangled black eyebrows. Nothing in the world pleases him—not even serving as commander of the Army of Mississippi. Not even starving out thousands of Union boys without firing so much as a shot.

He sits in the doorway of his tent reading reports from the field and sipping hot black coffee and smoking a cigar as short and big around as an eyebolt, but he takes no joy in any of it. The waiting strains his patience. It is a never-ending irritant, a fly buzzing untouchable within his brain. He sets down the sheaf of reports and calls to one of his lieutenants. The fellow approaches with the tentative steps of a man sent into a bullpen.

Bragg draws hungrily on the cigar, whose tip goes red and whose length diminishes by nearly a quarter of an inch in one draft. "Your report, Mickelson?" White smoke seethes from below his black mustache.

Mickelson salutes. "The scouts ain't back yet, sir."

"The war doesn't wait."

Mickelson risks a thin smile. "Nor do you, sir."

"Aye," says Bragg. "We are two sides of the same coin."

"One as impatient as the other."

"And every bit as insatiable." He pulls once more upon his cigar, and before dismissing Mickelson he shares with him an observation. "This siege business troubles me," he says. "There's no honor in it. A principled man would drown a sack of cats rather than leave them in a cage unfed, don't you think?"

The lieutenant can only agree. Nothing, however, will change.

When Mickelson's scouts do return, they are short one man. Murphy, the lovelorn boy, has run off. His partner claims not to know where they parted company or in which direction he headed, and although Mickelson has his doubts, there is no amount of interrogation or haranguing that will pry it out of him. He knows how to obtain the information he seeks but he would prefer not to involve General Bragg directly. Murphy is a good, strong Mississippi farm boy, tough and obedient and a dead shot with a rifle. He would hate to lose him.

Besides, Bragg will learn the truth in due time.

So he files his hasty report absent any mention of the deserter, and then he makes the rounds of the boy's unit, quietly buttonholing one man after another. He questions Murphy's bunkmates and his messmates and his every known associate, and in the end it is the young fiddler who suggests an excellent possibility. A girl named Sally, a town called Rossville, a romance. Mickelson rides out with a handful of men and they snatch him back before he has had a chance to plant so much as a kiss.

Bragg will preside over the court-martial. The preparations take the better part of a week. There is a jury box to be constructed, along with a witness stand for the use of those who are to testify and a bench from whose heights the general shall permit justice to rain down. There is to be seating provided for various other parties in two sets of bleachers, one on each side of the open-air courtroom. Every man not taking part in the proceedings will be required to bear witness and will do so on foot, at strict attention, in phalanx after orderly phalanx. Bragg is determined that it shall be an educational experience, a memorable lesson in Confederate discipline.

While the preparations go forward, Murphy languishes in a makeshift prison tent, chained to a mountain howitzer on loan from the artillery. He has but one visitor all week, the boy fiddler, who shakes his head and scuffs his boots on the dirt floor and denies all knowledge of the manner in which the army might have tracked him down. Murphy says it makes no difference to him—done is done, after all—but a rabid gleam in his eye suggests otherwise and makes the fiddler appreciate the chains that bind him and the quarter ton of bronze and cast iron to which they are attached. He keeps his distance and does not linger.

The court-martial begins at dawn and is a spectacle of the highest order, somber and flag bedecked. The weapons of the army ranked all around gleam and glint beneath the Tennessee sun. In another place and time these men might be Greeks massed before the gates of Troy— so much trouble laid at the feet of one woman, not Helen this time but Sally. The verdict is foregone, but in a show of decency or legal rectitude or perhaps just boredom General Bragg lets Murphy defend himself in detail and repent his crimes at length and ultimately plead for his life in the most abject of terms. A blind man—of which there are a handful in the camp, thanks to shrapnel and powder burns and moonshine whiskey—could see where the proceedings are headed.

The arguments and testimony draw to a close at last. Bragg charges the jury and orders the defendant returned to his canvas cell. He dismisses the rest of the men with orders to await a bugle call that will signal a decision, but no one leaves the field. To a man they set down their weapons and draw out their smoking implements and pass a few moments in subdued conversation rather than expend the energy required to walk off somewhere and be summoned right back. Their suspicions prove correct, and when the jury and the defendant return, they need only come to attention again to see this terrible business out.

The verdict, *guilty of desertion.*

The sentence, *death by fusillade.*

Bragg sets the execution for dawn, permitting Murphy an overnight period during which he might repent his sins, appeal to his Maker, and endure the sounds of dancing and fiddle music from around the campfire. Poor Jim does not feel much like playing when the appointed time arrives, and the willing dancers are few in number, for a suffocating pall has crept over the encampment. A fierce look from beneath the eyebrows of General Bragg, however, serves to set the gaiety in motion. The fiddler tunes up a little and tries his hand at "Soldier's Joy," slowing it to a crawl and setting it in a minor key as befits the occasion.

The road to Chattanooga runs through hell. It is barely a road at all, just sixty miles of mountain track, unimproved and untended. It is a narrow and twisted and ill-tempered thing of mudslides and boulders and deadfalls, littered with broken wagons and the corpses of horses. It is a thing far better suited to game than to man. Let it return to its native state when this infernal conflict is done. Let no civilized man ever have cause to travel it again.

They load Grant and his bad leg into the saddle before breakfast and they remove him and his bad leg at dusk, and between times the hard route tests his horsemanship without letup. At night he beds down under canvas with the rest of the party, sheltering against the rain that pours from the gunmetal sky. Between the thick clouds and the dense canopy of trees, even the stars hide themselves from this place.

He reminds himself from time to time that if the road were in better condition he would not be needing to travel it. Had fate provided a decent and direct way into the city—one not under Confederate control—his army would not be in this fix. His men would have food and ammunition and supplies, and they would not be at the mercy of Bragg's army. By night, more or less dry in his tent, he draws out his maps and searches by candlelight for some means, some miracle, by which he might release them from this fate.

Near midnight they stagger into Chattanooga under cover of a cold and heavy rain. The frame house that serves as the army's headquarters shows no sign of life beyond a single oil lamp burning in an upstairs window. Grant takes advantage of the darkness to let himself be lowered one last time from his horse. There is no need for these men to suspect that Lincoln has sent a crippled man to save them; the presence of his cane is indictment enough. He unships it from his saddlebag and leans upon it in the rain for a moment, drawing breath and girding himself, water spilling from the gutter of his hat. Then he goes to the house.

His knock draws an orderly in his nightshirt, a candle in hand. The young man yawns and blinks and gapes at the half-drowned figure before him. He looks like a man pulled from a river after some narrow escape.

From the wet darkness comes the rumble of a weary horseman's voice. "I reckon you ought to salute General Grant one of these days, son. Provided it ain't too much trouble."

Come morning, the skies have cleared. He steps out onto the porch of the white frame house and fills his lungs with the stench of ten thousand horses and mules starved to death and left to rot where they fell. The air is thick with their passing. He wonders how many men will meet the same fate. All of them, if the enemy has his way.

He saddles up and rides out alone to survey the town and the countryside around it. He squints into the early light and spies indications of the Army of Mississippi arrayed on the heights of Lookout Mountain and Missionary Ridge. He has seen these paired features so often on maps that he feels he knows them intimately. He looks upon them now from this low angle and senses himself and his men pinned within a bench vise about to be cranked shut. By all signs it is a case of starve or surrender, unless some third option proves possible. They lack the ammunition to endure so much as a single day's fighting.

The forests round about have been ravaged clean for firewood, leaving the landscape a sickly and stubbled waste. The horse clops along past squalid encampments where the men are more scarecrows than soldiers, all raw sinew and jutting bone, ill-clad and poorly shod if they are shod at all. Half rations have been the order for weeks. Grant's own belly rumbles with the eggs and ham he downed for breakfast, and he curses himself for his heartlessness. He was not thinking, when his only job is to think. He let himself believe that he had suffered privation on the journey over the mountain, when in truth he had known neither suffering nor privation. Not by comparison with these men.

He meets a certain William Farrar Smith in a desolate marshy spot beyond the town. Smith is a major general by rank and a Vermonter by birth and an engineer by inclination and assignment. Their paths first crossed at West Point. Such has been the case with so many of his coevals. They studied side by side and now they fight either that same way or tooth and nail instead. Stonewall and Lee and Pickett on the Rebel side, Sherman and Thomas and McClellan on the other. Many more as well. Even the foul-tempered Bragg took his training there. West Point was and is a factory for the manufacture of indiscriminate war, never mind the cause.

Grant and Smith, the general and the engineer, are of one mind. They have been working independently toward the same solution for a while now: a lifesaving supply line to be carved out between Bridgeport, Alabama, and this miserable valley of death. It will be a route partly overland and partly by water. There are roads to be cleared and temporary bridges to be laid and inconvenient Rebels to be slain or put to rout in the process. Others have previously considered this same work, General Thomas and the discredited Rosecrans in particular, but they have lacked the resolve or capacity to pursue it. Grant and Smith agree that it must be accomplished now.

"Stealthily and soon," says the engineer, "stealthily and soon." The words are a promise and a prayer.

———

What do you call the wrong side of a miracle?

It's not just bad luck; that much is certain. And it's far more than an arbitrary turn of events. Bragg believes that there is something *active* about it. A kind of evil intent.

One week ago, his scouts noted Grant's presence on the ground in Chattanooga. God knows where he'd come from or why an individual of his consequence would make an appearance at that doomed spot. They spied him on horseback, surveying the perimeter in the company of another officer, and in the respectful tradition of such matters they did not fire upon the two men but let them be. Today those same scouts report that the Union camp in the valley, an entire garrison, seems to have been resupplied.

Resupplied.

In full.

In one week's time.

What do you call the wrong side of a miracle?

Bragg kicks at the fire with the toe of his boot and watches the sparks circle upward. He lights a cigar, coughs, and curses bitterly to no one. If a miracle is an act of God, then the salvation of the Union presence in Chattanooga is the purest devilment. He would utter a prayer if he were a praying man. Why the Yankees lacked the decency to perish in the prescribed manner is beyond his understanding. Everything was arranged. Surely some dire force greater than Grant has interceded on their behalf.

A supply line has been cut through to Bridgeport, they say. Food and fodder, clothing and ammunition, supplies, both medical and otherwise, are flowing in like manna. He can only imagine the effect of such a thing upon the morale of the men. Grant may as well have parted the Red Sea on their behalf. They will do anything for him now.

It would be unlike the general to walk clean away at this point. More mischief is afoot. Bragg has no doubt of that.

What do you call the wrong side of a miracle?

He hasn't a word strong enough for it.

He thinks of the boy who deserted not so long ago. He was just one of a long and uninterrupted column of such figures, a cipher among much ciphering, inconsequential and practically nameless, useful chiefly for making a point. In serving that role he was exemplary. The general pulls on his cigar and weighs in his mind the value of the boy's life. He wonders if he would expend it in the same fashion today, or if he would instead have him take a Yankee bullet. Such are the dilemmas and responsibilities of leadership.

The advantage is lost before Bragg knows it. From withdrawal to retreat to utter bloody rout practically overnight. Everything slips away. It is as if a warhorse has put a single hoof wrong on a high shelf of brittle rock and loosed a mountain to crash down upon the Army of Mississippi.

It is no mountain. It is only Grant.

How many men lost? How many men broken? The accounting will be long and agonizing.

If only he had not delayed. War by strangulation did not suit him to begin with, and he half regrets it now. He could have ordered the siege ended with gunfire and death—different guns, anyhow, and different deaths. A victory instead of this disgrace. But now the town is lost. The valley is lost. Lookout Mountain and Missionary Ridge are lost. Lost and littered with the bodies of men and horses, fires burning everywhere as his army retreats. *Destroy anything of value* is the order of the day. Better to leave behind wreckage than to let the Union have the benefit of a cannon, a carton of shells, a blanket. Rifle fire weaves nettings of death along the slopes where his desperate men scramble toward a dream of safety. The very forest itself would seem to be on the attack. The trees burst and splinter, bark flying.

Time and fate have made deserters of them all. Perhaps, he thinks, they deserve no better than this. Himself included.

Grant's men take the armory at Chickamauga Station. Bragg has led them to it without meaning to, and they claim its riches as a bounty. Weapons, of course, and prisoners. Men who came here seeking refuge but have been denied it now. They make a ravaged lot, spent and hungry and chained to one another along the roadside like the very figures whose captivity they have fought to defend. Between bruise and blood and gunpowder, they are equally black.

A mounted line of Union officers draws closer in the dusk. They are hard used as well, and they sit on their horses in the way of invalids, stiffly and with a sort of wincing diffidence. Their eyes water from burnt powder and their ears ring with the echo of every shot fired over these last two days. They shall be hearing those echoes in their sleep, not only tonight but until death comes for each of them in his own time.

The prisoners ganged at the side of the road watch the officers resolve from the mist like lost souls on horseback. Two or three of them give looks resentful or defiant, but the rest just marvel that there are men other than themselves still walking the earth. Today's action should have been enough to strike down the entire race. They study their enemy, but what they see is hope.

"More mouths to feed," grumbles one of Grant's lieutenants, riding alongside the general toward the rear of the column.

"And more supplies with which to feed them," counters the general, showing an unexpected agreeableness.

The lieutenant goes on undeterred. "If a bullet had found every last one, we'd have less burden."

"Less burden upon our stores," says Grant, reining his horse a bit. "But more upon our souls. You seem to forget that we are here to save

50

the Union, not to slaughter boys from Mississippi. We shall need them when we are reunited."

Grant falls back from the lieutenant, positioning himself last in the column. He adjusts his collar and backhands a streak of dust from his pant leg. Then, as his horse comes abreast of the ragged line of chained and exhausted men, he lifts his hat in a long show of brotherhood.

There is no man among them who does not know him on sight. There is no man among them who will ever forget his passage down that darkening road.

Forty Days and Forty Nights

The brownstone on Sixty-Sixth Street has grown ten times, a hundred times, a thousand times larger. If you tried to map it all, unreeling a cord behind you in the Cretan manner, you would never find its limits. Halls open onto longer halls. Doors — in plain sight and hidden — lead to other spaces, other floors, other realities entirely. Each window opens onto its own weather, its own season, its own hour of the day or night.

A place this unsettling ought to be thronged with ghosts, and it is. The brownstone on Sixty-Sixth Street is every bit as haunted as Grant's own brain. In its numberless kitchens, men from the Sanitary Commission dole out salt pork, boiled potatoes, and hardtack. The elbows of aproned surgeons drip blood and other, more mysterious fluids into every available sink and toilet and tub. Each bedroom and dining room and reception space is crowded rank on rank with men sleeping on cots and on provisional pallets and on the cold bare floor.

In his own study — or one of his several studies, for he seems to have encountered a half dozen of them at least — a council of war is underway. Presiding is a figure who from certain angles resembles Lincoln and from others looks quite like Grant himself. The rest of the men are unknown to him. He clears his throat and sniffs a time or two and finally raps upon the desk to get their attention, but he must seem to these haunts a haunt himself. Only one of the men present, a supercilious fellow drawing on a pipe whose smoke is a shade more translucent than his own flesh, seems to notice anything curious. He twists his neck and swats at the air with his free hand. *Damned flies.*

A clanking from the kitchen draws Grant's attention. Some spirit of a more conventional, chain-rattling sort, he decides. Rather than wait until the thing materializes behind his back or in a dim corner of his vision, he leaves the study and hurries down the hallway toward the sound. Better to brave such a thing than to be caught unawares by it.

In the kitchen he discovers not a ghost but a familiar face: his valet, Harrison Terrell, in the flesh and sorting cutlery. What a delight! What a comfort! Trust Faithful Harrison to take on more than his regular duties should the remainder of the staff go missing or discarnate.

"Mr. Grant, sir?" The man's voice contains traces of his native Virginia. Grant finds comfort in that too. His manner of speaking conjures up the past, although it is not a specific past that the two of them share directly. He has been on the staff for only a handful of years. He entered Grant's life practically in tandem with the house, and he has been close to the heart of it ever since.

Grant knows precious little about him. He knows that he was born into slavery in Virginia and that he was a beneficiary of the Emancipation. He knows that he learned his current business serving the eminent banker George Washington Riggs of Washington and that he came to Grant as highly recommended as a servant could possibly be.

Terrell, by contrast, knows things about his employer that even Julia does not. Precisely how many cigars he smokes each day. What articles of the mail he must have right off and which are not worth carrying to the study. How he prefers his tie knotted. Which pairs of trousers grow snug around the waist if he has been too long at the table.

Such bits of information that Grant has inadvertently learned about Terrell have come by way of Julia, who generally acquires them from the cook, who usually learns them from one of the chambermaids, who picks them up by way of an overheard conversation between Terrell and the gardener. Like every great enterprise, the brownstone on Sixty-Sixth Street has a complex and fully operational grapevine telegraph. A person cannot help but know one or two things.

Grant understands that Harrison has a wife and one son. The son—and this he got straight from the banker Riggs—is in Massachusetts, studying at the Groton School of all places. Grant suspects that Riggs used his influence to arrange his admission, but Riggs has kept diplomatically mum on the subject. Grant doesn't mind. He is just glad to see that the postwar world is still so full of miracles.

"Mr. Grant," Harrison says again, placing a handful of cutlery on the countertop and pressing the drawer closed with his hip. "What can I do for you?"

Grant opens his mouth to make some kind of answer, but nothing comes out. Terrell touches his shoulder in a subtle, steadying way and reaches to the table for a pencil and a scrap of paper. "Sir? If you'd like?"

And he is back in the cottage once more. The counter behind Harrison is the correct counter and the table before him is the correct table and the cursed pencil and paper are the same as well. Every one of them disappoints him. Better Sixty-Sixth Street than here. Better a haunted brownstone than this borrowed cottage made of silence and ruin.

After a moment he takes up the pencil and paper. Leaning heavily on the counter, he summons all his strength and scratches out a message. *Harrison*, it says. *Only you.*

Terrell reads it aloud, pinches his lower lip, nods. "Oh, yes, Mr. Grant," he says. "I'm the only one home just now. Mrs. Grant and the children and the grandchildren decided to take their luncheon at the hotel. They promised to bring something back for you and me, though. That was Mrs. Grant's idea."

The general still looks a trifle disoriented, but Terrell takes him by his waist and his elbow and helps him back to his chair. There he deposits him as gently as he would settle his own child.

CHAPTER 5

1865

City Point

High upon a bluff over the James River, he awaits the arrival of three peace commissioners from the Confederacy. They are here to await a summons from Lincoln, who is on his way to Hampton Roads for the occasion. They come beneath a white flag and under false pretenses. Grant cannot see it any other way. They seem to him characters out of one of Shakespeare's comedies, foolish representatives of a thing that does not even exist—the Confederate States—bent on negotiating terms with a thing that most assuredly does, the United States of America. The affair is ridiculous on its face, an absolute charade, but he must behave as if the fate of the Union will depend upon it. Perhaps it will. That shall be for Lincoln to decide.

As for him, he would prefer to accept the surrender of a proper army. That would be a thing with meaning, a thing that bore weight. These pompous marionettes with their white flag and their civilian clothes do not deserve to be taken seriously. They ought to be treated like the insurrectionists they are, taken prisoner and questioned, although not one of them would hold up under five minutes' interrogation. Rules are rules, though, and customs are customs, and orders are above all orders.

He is in his quarters atop the bluff, working by lamplight and firelight, when distant cheers signal the emissaries' passage across Union lines. Julia hears the commotion first, and she goes to the window. What a joy it has been to have her here! Julia and her reliable Jule, together as in the days of their youth. Julia's touch will be felt here long after she returns home to Missouri, her presence preserved by the gingham curtains she has hung in the windows, the framed ambrotypes she has arranged on the mantelpiece, the colorful linens she has set out in the adjoining officers' mess. This log cabin conjures Hardscrabble in any number of ways, and everything about it makes him feel young again. Vigorous and full of life in this place of life's denial.

He has ordered a steamship secured at the landing as temporary quarters for the three visitors. Chief among them will be Alexander Stephens, vice president of the Confederacy. He has seen images of the man before, and he is not expecting much. Stephens has always seemed a trifle small and fragile, boyish in his looks, perhaps even a bit fey in his bearing. One would think him not exactly the best that the Rebels could find to serve as second-in-command of their not-quite-nascent government. On the other hand, Lincoln has known him for twenty years and has nothing but praise for his character. So be it, then. The general must try to keep an open mind, but he feels no obligation to be sociable.

A knock comes at the cabin door, followed by the low voice of one of his lieutenants. It is the delegation, come to pay their respects before reporting to their temporary quarters. Grant coughs and calls out to admit them but does not stir from his table. Julia vanishes behind the Indian blanket that serves to partition off the bedroom.

The door swings wide upon the night. They stand in a tight tableau, silhouetted as one against the night sky, as alike as tenpins and as closely arranged. He could roll a cannonball and knock them all down. He wonders which one might be Stephens, or if there has been some change of plans and a man of larger scale has been substituted.

His lieutenant steps into the lamplit cabin and the delegation follows. A little wind arises and they blow in upon it, the last man closing the door and securing it behind him. Grant has not yet moved from his desk or even granted them his attention. His pen scratches away. The lieutenant greets the general and the general acknowledges him with a curt nod. There is a row of pegs on the wall just inside the door and the general indicates them and watches from under his eyebrows as the men begin to remove their hats and coats.

It proves a revelation.

One of the delegates is bundled in a kind of long overcoat that Grant has seen only once or twice before. It is a new design of Southern manufacture, built for wear in northern climes far more forbidding than the lowlands of Virginia. Grant smiles to himself at the optimism inherent in it. The Confederates must now envision themselves marching victorious all the way to the North Pole. The fabric is a dense gray wool, thick as bull hide and every bit as stiff. It has a tall, generous collar and reinforced shoulders and a short cape to repel the weather, and it drapes fully to the toes of the figure within it. The coat has the grace and mass of an igloo, and the man who emerges from its depths proves no match for it once he is out.

It is Stephens, restored to his ordinary dimensions. The man has proven to be all shuck and no ear, and Grant would know him anyplace.

A stifled gasp from behind the Indian blanket indicates that Julia has seen his transformation as well.

The little man hands his great drooping coat to his lieutenant, turns again to Grant, and raises an eyebrow. "I wonder which of the two Julias might be in the next room, General."

Grant stiffens.

"Would it be your wife? Or your wife's girl? I understand they travel together."

"They do." If Stephens means to use this contradiction as a bargaining chip of some sort, he will be disappointed.

"The circumstance is widely known."

"I suspect that it is," says Grant. "We make no secret of it."

"I'm told that it has even come to Lincoln's attention."

"President Lincoln is not blind."

"They say he receives disapproving correspondence on the subject."

"He does not mention it to me. Our communications have to do with the war."

Stephens smiles the smile of a man not entirely thwarted. Not yet.

"If you think Mrs. Grant's choice in companions may be employed to discredit me," says the general, "I invite you to make the attempt. The girl belongs to neither of us. She is the property of my father-in-law, and she attends Mrs. Grant at his bidding."

"Very well," says Stephens in a kind of withdrawal. "In any event, I assure you that I ask from curiosity, not from ill intent."

Grant smiles. "Oh, you're very much entitled to ill intent. I should depend upon it. But a proper statesman would keep it better concealed."

The remainder of the visit is civil, cordial, and entirely without consequence. Grant guides the talk to their travels, not their plans. He would no more discuss politics or war with these gentlemen than he would discuss spiritualism with a mule. They represent no government that he recognizes. As a result, he impresses the delegation as a man who knows more than he says, a man content to keep his own counsel.

When they have taken their leave, with the miniature vice president of their sham government concealed once more beneath his overcoat, Julia comes from the bedroom. Her husband sits at his table, paperwork ignored, lost in thought, and she goes to him. "How insolent that little fellow was," she says, her voice low.

Ulysses nods. "It's poor manners," he says, "and worse strategy."

"The nerve of that Confederate, to disapprove of our having Jule."

"People do."

She takes a seat. "It's no concern of theirs."

"Perhaps not."

"Do they suppose we mistreat her?"

"It's common enough. I'm sure Stephens's people treat their own a good deal worse."

"They must think you a hypocrite to be fighting this war. They must think me one as well."

"What another man thinks—what our enemy thinks—is no matter. My charge is to bind up the nation they've broken in two, not to soften their hearts regarding the black man."

Forty Days and Forty Nights

Whether injected into his bloodstream or applied directly to his throat, the compounds prescribed by Dr. Douglas have the power to open doors in his mind. He remembers everything, and if he is not careful he might remember more.

One place, one time—they bleed into a different place and different time. From the cottage at Mount McGregor to the cabin at City Point, from this night to a night many years previous.

He has instructed Jule to bank the fire, and together he and Julia have retired. Jule fetches her tick mattress and threadbare blanket to the kitchen, makes up her bed as near the stove as she dares, and puts out the candles. Night closes in, black and silent as an early grave, but her eyes and ears adjust to it. She has learned in this life of hers to adjust to almost anything.

A horse whinnies now and then, and from the river beyond the bluff a rhythmic creaking sound drifts upward. A dim light floats by at some distance now and then, vague and ghostly. A man standing guard, likely, although against what she cannot say. With the bluff jutting over the river to the east and the Union army massed in every other direction, they are perfectly safe. The general would not bring Mrs. Grant to a place that was otherwise.

Sleep, though she has earned it, comes hard. She counts sheep until she reaches her limit, and then she counts again. She studies the drifting of that outer light, and she pictures the soldier out there on his rounds, and she attempts to be hypnotized by the slow rhythm of it all. To sink into it as into someone else's dream of someone else's feather bed. She thinks on her brothers, back home at White Haven, their work more taxing than hers but her loneliness greater. At least they have one another.

General Grant begins to snore. Before long Mrs. Grant joins in, more softly but with a vexing irregularity. Together they make a duet less pleasing than a person might like, but it is no business of hers. She presses one ear against the straw tick and stoppers the other with the blanket, but it does no good. It leaves her feet uncovered besides.

She considers the fragile barrier between the inside of this cabin and the great world beyond it. The door has no lock. The windows do not latch. The general and his wife are sleeping. She could slip out into the night with no one the wiser. This cabin seems to her a soap bubble in the wind, an egg in the ocean, some small and fragile thing afloat within a limitless and powerful one.

But where would she go? Out of Virginia. North, into the unknown.

And how far would she get? No farther than that guard with his pistol and his lamp. Past him is the high bluff. Past that, the river. And arrayed in every other direction is the army—an army at war with the idea of slavery but tolerant of its practice. Escape is impossible. She would draw no more than a handful of unencumbered breaths, and their price would be an early return to White Haven. There, Colonel Dent would be free to work his will.

Grant awakens at Mount McGregor, dreaming that he is awakening at City Point. As the fog clears, there is an unreality about the whole business in either case, a quality of the temporary and provisional. Neither cottage nor cabin belongs to him, after all. He is a wayfaring stranger with no real home in this world—not even, it would seem, within his own body. How else to explain this dream of dreaming, this dream of awakening, this dream of inhabiting a foreign consciousness—the consciousness of a woman, and a black one at that?

CHAPTER 6

1862

Revelations

Two recent deaths at White Haven have given the colonel a new appreciation for the black man, and he doesn't mind telling Ulysses and Julia about it over breakfast. "If I lose another one," he says, "I don't know how we'll get by."

The first to give up the ghost was Old Joe Tyson, a bent-backed ancient handy with a scythe and handier still with a draw knife when there was call for it. He could clear a field or bark a tree faster than a man half his age. He died in the spring, of his own antiquity.

The second was William Monroe, who'd crossed the Jordan with his whole life ahead of him. He was a tough customer who'd once gotten the idea of running off, and he had a back full of welts to help him remember his mistake. A month ago he'd been taking down a shagbark hickory under the direction of Elwood Marshall, and the hired man had miscalculated the angles. Another valuable piece of property, gone in an instant.

"I'd have taken the loss out of Marshall's pocketbook," says the colonel, "but I don't pay him that kind of money. I can't take it out of his hide, either. Useless as he is, I need him upright."

"Oh, Father," says Julia. "What shall you do?"

"For now, I shall continue to hang by a thread. I'd be in a far better position, of course, if I could persuade those present to pull their own weight." To judge from the look he gives his son-in-law, by *present* he would seem to mean *right at this very table.*

Grant would remind him that this visit is for Julia's benefit only, that they have undertaken it at some cost and inconvenience, and that, as commanding general of the army, he has responsibilities other than digging post holes and mucking out stalls. But he says nothing. He has learned that if he should call the weather fine, the colonel will make a show of fetching his raincoat.

When they are finished they go their separate ways—Dent into his office, Julia and Ulysses out into the morning—leaving the breakfast things to Jule.

Wife and husband set out down the lane. They mean to take a long way home to Hardscrabble. It has been so many months since Julia was last here, and she is so refreshed by the familiar sights and smells and sounds, that she wants to take in every stalk of grain, every apple, every atom.

"Oh, Ulys," she says. "To imagine that this could all be lost . . ."

"Why should it be lost?"

"For the want of one more Negro."

"Nonsense," says Grant. "Men like Monroe and Tyson are easy enough to replace. And it's possible your father has more resources than he lets on."

"Do you think so?"

He shrugs. "What bothers him more is that two of his prized possessions were bold enough to die."

"Now, now. He mourns them as anyone would."

Grant frowns. "Perhaps. Perhaps he only mourns the loss of his property."

"I suppose so," says Julia. "Sentiment has never made a dent in him."

Her husband seizes on a chance to lighten the mood. "A *dent*, you say? Why, the man is nothing but Dent."

"Oh, Ulys."

"He is Dent from head to toe."

Julia laughs. "All right. It's never made an *impression*, then."

"Fair enough." They walk on and he opens a gate and admits her first. They proceed hand in hand into a field of tall grass with an apple orchard beyond it. As they go, he decides that as far as the colonel is concerned, the two slaves may as well have run off. Dent must take it for the most terrible sin a Negro can possibly commit: an act of free will. He makes no mention of it.

Julia returns to the original question. "What if you're wrong about his finances," she says, "and White Haven is truly in peril?"

"He could sell off land. He'd have less property to manage and more funds for handling it."

"Of course! Then he could acquire a new man. Replace Monroe."

"He could do that. If he insists on falling back on the old ways."

"They're the only ways he knows. Besides, you sound like an abolitionist."

Grant pulls up short at the edge of the orchard. "I don't care much for abolition one way or the other. You know that. My concern is putting down the Rebellion."

"But you've grown so disapproving, Ulys."

Her husband nods, considers. "Perhaps I have," he says at last, "and if I have spoken out of turn, I regret it. But you see, it's not that I dislike the business of slavery so much; it's that your father is so damnably attached to it. Slavery is doomed. Its eradication will leave him penniless. History will leave him behind."

The idea further solidifies in the dark hours just before morning. Julia is asleep alongside him. Jule is downstairs, on a pallet laid out in a corner of the kitchen. It is an acknowledgment of her long history and special standing.

He has been up half the night, thinking about his wife, about Jule, and about the two lost black men. He has been thinking about Missouri, an exasperating place torn between slaveholding and abolition, secession and union. He has been thinking mostly, however, about his father-in-law. How tied the man is to a practice deemed intolerable by so many of his countrymen. How accustomed he is to thinking himself utterly superior to the members of an entire race. How disastrous the loss of that race's compelled labor would be to him and to his possessions and to his way of life.

The colonel will never yield, and neither will any other man in the Confederacy, so he sees it all at once: to win the war without having to slaughter every last Rebel there is, the Union must break their spirits and drain their resources. Abolition is a tool to that end, no matter how little he cares for its underpinnings in the rights of man. The rights of man have no bearing in wartime, no use beyond the strategic. So although the disposition of the slave population counts for very little in his mind and heart, he shall from now on make common cause with his abolitionist brothers. It will aid in reuniting the nation. It will help break the back of the Rebel economy. It will redouble his own confidence in victory.

He wakes in the glow of dawn, and at the same time Julia stirs to the scents rising from the kitchen. Ham and redeye gravy over buttermilk biscuits. Coffee too. God bless Jule. What would they do without her?

Forty Days and Forty Nights

The injection slips into his bloodstream and his consciousness drifts away upon it. Exactly what combination of dangerous anesthetics and unlikely cures and raw intoxicants it might contain does not concern him. Brandy, chloroform, cocaine, laudanum, morphine—it is all one to the patient and all one to the cancer within him.

Downstream he floats toward a memory, if it could be called that. A memory slipped free and forgotten or not even registered to start with. A memory that he owns at second hand if he owns it at all.

A knock at an unseen door awakens him from concentration so deep that it could pass for oblivion. He looks up and rubs his eyes and discovers that he is in his office, his old office at the White House. He straightens his shoulders and breathes deeply and without pain. He touches his collar and he tugs at the tie knotted there and his throat does not cry out in protest. A miracle. How far back has he drifted? How long vanished is this world he inhabits? Fifteen years, perhaps. Surely not much more.

It is the blink of an eye.

It is a lifetime.

The presidency—trials and obstacles and all—seems an Eden to him now.

The lightly curtained windows admit gauzy sunlight and a mild breeze. Any number of priceless paintings—battle scenes, landscapes, solemn portraits of men who have occupied this office in years gone by—decorate the walls. Nearer to hand, the desk holds a small collection of cherished mementos, along with papers stacked and sorted so meticulously that one might think his work here straightforward. He feels himself accustomed once again to such order, never mind what has happened in life since the moment he now inhabits. Order was essential during the War of the Rebellion and the years of his presidency. Since then, everything has been a losing battle against entropy and decay.

A knock comes upon the door, followed almost immediately by the personage of William M. Stewart. The senator from Nevada has not bothered to wait for an answer but barges in as if he has been put in charge of things. He drags behind him a younger man, an unimpressive, rail-thin rag doll dressed like a cowhand got up for Sunday.

A constituent, no doubt, seeking some indulgence. A tradesman fallen on hard times, a prospector come up empty-handed. Grant casts his eye upon him for a second and then looks down at the papers arrayed on his desk. It is clear that he has much to do and little time for pleasantries, but there is no harm in making a man feel welcome, is there? Besides, finding himself restored to these opulent rooms and this excellent health, he might enjoy an exchange with a visitor or two.

Stewart drags the fellow across the room and stands him up before the president's desk. The younger man possesses the beginnings of a mustache and is possessed by a wayward eruption of red hair. His shirtsleeves are smeared with black, and his hands are smeared as well, and there are smudges of it on his cheekbones and his forehead.

By the look of it, he has been wrestling with an inkpot. This does not trouble the president in the least, for he has found himself in states less tidy a thousand times. At Appomattox Courthouse, most memorably, where Lee surrendered his army to an unprepossessing Ohioan clad in the uniform—and the mud, and the exhaustion, and the gladness—of a common soldier. Clothing and cleanliness carry little weight in his mind.

"Mr. President," says the senator, "I'd like to introduce a young fellow from Nevada. He'll be helping in my office for a bit."

"I'm glad to hear it, Senator."

"Paperwork, you know. That sort of thing."

"Ah," says Grant, sizing up the red-haired man. "He looks cut out for that sort of work, doesn't he?"

The fellow suppresses a smile. He might have dodged that bullet or returned fire, but he is at too close range.

"Oh, he is," says Stewart. "He is mighty handy with a pen."

"There's never been any harm in that, I suppose, except to a man's clothing." He can see that the fellow is comfortable with the joshing, rough-and-tumble ways of workingmen—whether on the farm, in the factory, or on the field of battle. He is reminded of a thousand unassuming good fellows he has known in the past. "Senator Stewart represents a very young state," he says. "You must have been born somewhere else."

"Missouri, Mr. President. But I lit out as quickly as I could."

"I left Ohio the very same way," says Grant. "Bound for your Missouri, as it happens."

"I trust you weren't as disappointed by the place as I was."

"Far from it. I found my wife there," says Grant.

"Then the trip was wisely undertaken."

Grant nods. "And you? What have you found in the wilderness, besides Senator Stewart?"

"A change of scenery, Mr. President. And honest work, and a great many marvelous stories to tell."

Stewart leans in. "Mr. Clemens is quite accomplished in that line. He has been in all the newspapers." He looks proud enough to have written the jumping frog story himself.

Long-suffering Grant, emerging in a fog from this reverie or dream, will shake his head and scratch an ear and swallow painfully against the cancer in his throat, whose raucous protestations will remind him of exactly where he is and when. He does not recall his introduction to Clemens going this way at all. His picture of the occasion is different—a memory surely given him by Clemens himself. Clemens has repeated the story many times, in public and private, retelling it as a brief and hesitant meeting of two quite similar minds. According to his version, they uttered little more than a dozen words between them, one sentence each, but those sentences served as both a bit of tentative badinage and the foundation of endless conversations to come.

Grant recalls no such circumstance. So blank is his memory—until now he hasn't even recalled the existence of a Senator Stewart, much less any role the Nevadan might have played—that for years he has had to humor Clemens by pretending to remember the occasion. It is good for his friend's self-regard, and it costs him nothing.

CHAPTER 7

1865

The Package—Part One

His tailor in Richmond receives the order by messenger and takes it for an omen, although exactly what it might mean is beyond guessing. A person could draw from it a hundred shaded distinctions, and only one of them matters in the end. Victory or surrender. The rest are filigree.

It is to be a magnificent suit of clothing. The instructions, infinitely detailed and accompanied by line drawings done in a fine hand, arrived with a bolt of the highest-quality English wool and a purchase order signed by Major J. B. Ferguson. Ferguson is well-known in these parts. He and the tailor shared many a boyhood frolic and many a youthful rivalry and many a businessman's fine bottle of claret right here in this charming Southern city—until Ferguson was called off to London to aid in provisioning the army. He is a major now, head of the quartermasters, and his signature on a document like this one is an ironclad guarantee of payment.

The tailor runs the fabric between his thumb and forefinger, anticipating how each panel will fall and drape. In his mind's eye the garments are as good as made. The order calls for a frock coat, a waistcoat, and trousers. Also a formal red sash, to be made from local materials of the very finest quality. Every braid and button and scrap of embroidery is laid out precisely and to the tightest of tolerances. The tailor compares these measurements to those of the most recent outfit he has made for the individual in question—it was another full-dress uniform, similar in style but cut from more common cloth—and he discerns from the differences that the war has taken a toll on the man's body. He has lost some weight, when he had little to spare. His stance remains upright, though, and he is still as long in the leg and square in the shoulder as he ever was. What a figure he shall cut.

The tailor sets all of his other work aside. He locks the door, hangs a placard in the window, and lowers the stenciled shade. For a week he labors alone in the dim filtered light, the vision of the uniform leading him on like a talisman raised before an enslaved army of one. His hands fly. His eyes burn. The tips of his fingers roughen and bleed. His wife brings his meals to the rear door and leaves them on a table there beneath a checkered napkin. She never spies him, she never sees so much as his shadow, but when she returns she finds his plates emptied and scoured clean as if by an overnight visitation of elves.

In seven days the miracle is done.

A messenger appears at the stroke of noon. The man's rank is mysterious to the tailor, who ought to know it at a glance. He seems in fact to have been invented for this purpose only. He says he is here for the uniform, and when the tailor hesitates, he produces his orders. The tailor folds the uniform as meticulously as he would fold Communion linens, and then folds it all over again to make some invisible improvement in his work. He wraps the result in tissue paper and ties it off. Then he wraps it once more, in butcher paper this time, and ties it off again. Finally, still not quite satisfied, he pulls down from a dusty shelf a suitable piece of waterproof canvas and wraps it all a third time, as if readying a treasure for some difficult ocean voyage. He ties it off with a length of rope.

"No need to address it," says the messenger as he signs the receipt. "It ain't going by regular mail."

———

To Robert E. Lee, this season of the war has about it a smell of endings. The conflict has dragged on long enough. The men who are not dead are sick and the men who are not sick are dispirited. The same goes for both sides; he is certain of that. No brawl can continue for this long and yield a civilized outcome. The thing will be decided not by one side's superiority but by the other side's tolerance for its own destruction.

And it is not just the men who will one day yield. The earth herself has endured over these past four years abuse so terrible that she may never recover. Her forests have been cut down one minié ball at a time, leaving the very ground planted with leaden death. What wickedness may grow there? Her fields have been trampled flat and nourished with the indistinguishable blood of men and horses. What evil may rise up from their furrows? Her footpaths and game trails have been paved over with the broken and burnt components of every kind of lumbering war machine. What horrors may be mined from their depths?

He wonders exactly what will be the result of bringing the war to a close. One can hardly expect sudden amity to spring up among people who have spent the last four years murdering one another. The nation will be altered, surely—the institution of slavery will live or die, at least in the lawbooks—but the hearts of the nation will go on as they always have. And whether it is the Confederacy or the Union that goes down to defeat, the result will be the same. The chief issue will appear settled, but it will not be settled. One man's instinct to control another man— whether the other is a genteel planter in a place so far away as to exist in a different world, or a black slave marooned upon these shores with no possible future but poverty and ignorance—will remain unchastened and unimproved. Man is forever yearning to be God, and he can be counted upon to fail every time.

The general envisions the coming occasion not as a victory or a surrender, then, but as a cessation of the most blatant and organized of the hostilities. That will have to be enough.

He has requisitioned a new uniform against the day. Whether he will be dictating terms or accepting them, he means to be outfitted with dignity.

The package is traded hand to hand all the way from Richmond. It travels by carriage and wagon and cart, in company that grows heavier and rougher by the mile. Private correspondence and delicate edibles, kitchen goods and medical supplies, homespun clothing and hard liquor, cornmeal and horse blankets, gunpowder and lead. All that it bears by way of address is "Gen. Robt. E. Lee—Army of Northern Virginia." Even this late in the war, that makes it a moving target. Its path resembles the course of a worm tunneling blind through rotten wood, or a lightning bolt chasing itself from cloud to cloud.

The package arrives with the morning's field intelligence, and he knows it by its dimensions and weight despite its wrappings of sailcloth. The tailor was correct to bundle it so. Over these last days it has passed through a war, and it bears all the marks. It has been splashed with mud and horse shit and black coffee. It has been folded in half and jammed between cartons of ammunition to still their infernal rattling. It has

been soaked in a spray of arterial blood and a drip of something me-
dicinal, likely iodine. And it has broken the fall of at least one drunken
soldier, in an act of kindness neither dreamed of nor approved by its
eventual recipient.

Lee has such faith in the quartermasters that he does not so much as
try the uniform on. To do so would be a sort of betrayal and might even
tempt fate. The garment has a mysterious power, a significance that can
be neither calculated nor conjured until the moment is right. It will be a
revelation. So he does not even unwrap it but stows it untouched in his
trunk. The package takes up more room than he'd like, and it stinks of
the troubles it's been through. He would put it beneath a blanket under
his cot, but the army is on the move now, constantly on the move, and
he must not risk losing track of it.

The tailor goes back to his daily round, but the work gives him little joy.
No fabric feels in his hand half so soft and supple as the gray wool supplied for Lee's uniform. No garment seems as perfectly proportioned as the
general's slightly-narrower-than-previous frock coat. No lapel lies as flat,
no buttonhole cooperates as amenably, no lining drapes with such grace.

He still has a bit of the English wool left over, just a yard and a little
more, and he ponders what he ought to do with it. There is simply not
enough to sew anything worthy of the raw material. Cutting it, piercing
it with needles, assailing its perfection in any way for so small a gain
would be a sin. Best to leave it alone. So he folds it into a flat box and
seals the box against moths with a glued paper strip and sets it in a place
of honor on the highest shelf.

He tells everyone he meets about the commission, and with each
telling the uniform improves. It becomes a garment for a conqueror or

a king. He regrets that he did not have the chance to hang it in his shop window for even a day or two, because it would have guaranteed his reputation forever. Now it lives only as a legend, a rumor, and the tailor himself is brought once again to hemming trousers and adjusting waistbands. One day, he fears, he shall be reduced to converting window dressings into ball gowns.

Often he closes the shop early, exhausted by the pettiness of the work he must do to make ends meet, and he hastens down to the tavern on the corner. It is a dim place, narrow and cramped and full of smoke. It is frequented equally by locals and traveling men visiting the capital on trade or legal business. He has friends here and he makes more. He grows garrulous as he drinks. He claims to know how the war will end, and he makes himself a public authority on the subject.

"The Confederacy is about to triumph," he says. "I can tell you that as plain as day."

A pale-haired gentleman with a neat mustache and a double whiskey fixes him with a look. "Tell me more," he says. "Are you in possession of some crystal ball?" The man is clearly not from these parts. His accent is untraceable. He could be a prospector bound for the frontier or a visitor from Europe or a Yankee spy.

It makes no difference to the tailor. His story is the same no matter who hears it. The detailed order from Major J. B. Ferguson. The magnificent English wool provided with it. The precise measurements and the splendid resultant uniform—a garment fit to be worn at a coronation. It can signify only one thing, a garment that fine. Lee is fixing to make fast a Confederate victory, and he means to look the part on the occasion of Grant's surrender.

"How much did they give you for the whole package?" asks the mustached gentleman, a question that reveals him to be a man of business.

The tailor names the amount.

The gentleman's face betrays shock.

"Yes, sir," says the tailor, proud of himself. "And I have the purchase order to prove it. That much and not a penny less."

"For a garment that beautifully made? For a garment of such historic importance? Why, sir, I daresay that you have been had."

The tailor puts down his glass and collects his thoughts.

"Oh, yes," says the gentleman. "You've been cheated for certain."

"Nonsense," says the tailor. "You don't know my business."

"I know the value of things."

The tailor studies his glass but makes no dispute.

"Have you sent your bill?"

"I shall in a week's time, when the month ends."

"Double it."

"Ridiculous."

"Isn't the uniform worth that much? Perhaps more?"

"I suppose it is."

"Then you mustn't give it away. It's bad business."

The tailor cogitates.

"A victorious Confederacy will think nothing of it. They'll be happy to pay. I'd wager you'll be something of a celebrity."

The tailor's eyes brighten in the dim tavern light. "I suppose I'll never get it if I don't ask."

"That's the spirit," says the traveling gentleman.

Forty Days and Forty Nights

He is waiting at the station in Nashville.

He *was* waiting.

He is waiting.

The war is almost over but mankind's troubles are not. The general, for example, is right now bound most urgently for home. The train cannot arrive soon enough to suit him, and once he is on board it will wait too long in departing. He swears that if he could command it to speed on through without so much as stopping, he would gather all his anguished strength and leap aboard from the roadbed. There is no time to waste.

His eldest son, Fred, is home at Hardscrabble in the grip of typhoid. The boy is no doubt growing weaker by the moment, and other than a slave nurse on loan from Dent he is all alone in his suffering, for his mother is traveling too. The general, thanks to distress and failing memory and the fog of history that he inhabits, does not recall exactly where. They are both traveling, though—this much he knows—and their courses are to converge in St. Louis. A military escort will be waiting there to carry them home.

In his mind's eye, in his imagination, in a dream induced by opium and its abettors, he sees his beloved approaching her own train. She is followed closely by the constant Jule. The slave woman deals with the porters and the conductors and the stowed luggage, tucking the receipts into the pocket of her apron. She makes the climb up the little flight of iron steps a half dozen times lest they leave some trifle behind.

Julia, unencumbered, vanishes into the car. So it has always been.

The general sees them settle alongside each other in the seats of a passenger car and he should doubt the evidence of his fabricating eye, but he does not. A lounge car it ought to be, but the change makes no difference to the narrative about to unfold.

He sees the landscape passing outside their window. He feels Julia wishing that the train would go faster and he feels Jule wishing that it would stop dead forever and ever, amen. They are heading for Missouri, a border state where the Emancipation Proclamation has yet to take hold. They are headed home.

The train stops in Louisville to take on passengers and mail. There is to be a delay of some half hour, during which Julia will remain fastened to her seat. The tiniest creak or shudder startles her and causes her to tighten her grip on the windowsill, beyond which a great human bustling goes on.

Jule is all nerves as well. She perspires and dabs at her forehead with a kerchief. She asks permission to lower the window an inch to admit some fresh air, but she is not comforted by the result. She finds a printed schedule and fans herself with it as if otherwise she must surely die.

"Why don't you step out onto the platform?" says her mistress.

"Oh, no, ma'am. I couldn't."

"It's only for a moment."

"But I mustn't."

"If I say you must, then you must."

Jule fans herself desperately. "I'll be fine. We'll be leaving soon."

"Not as soon as all that. I insist that you go."

Jule rises halfway.

"Go now."

Jule looks longingly toward the rear door.

"Take a moment," says Julia. "Hurry back, is all."

"Yes, ma'am." And she goes.

Time passes, and the great tumult beyond the window gives no sign of slowing. Workmen struggle with great sacks of mail and porters manhandle groaning steamer trunks. Conductors, armed with impatient good cheer, sort passengers into cars: those with beaver hats and starched shirts and neckties go this way, those in sturdy trousers and rope galluses and work boots go that.

Julia closes her eyes and clears her mind and feels the pounding of her heart. The poor weary thing pumps enough lifeblood for two, just as it did when Fred's unformed self dwelled within her. Fifteen years ago that was, and the connection shall never be severed or even diminished. She thinks, as she tries not to think at all, that it might in fact be her own maternal heartbeat, two states distant, in a steam train paused for reasons of its own, that keeps Fred safely suspended above the abyss of death.

From beyond the window, at an angle so steep as to render her nearly invisible against the train, Jule cranes her neck and takes note. Her mistress cannot possibly be sleeping. Some other woman might—left alone and in momentary peace along this dread journey—but not Mrs. Julia Dent Grant. She knows her better than that, and well she should.

She smiles at a porter and offers him the receipt for her little case.

He studies the paper for a moment and smiles back and advises her that this station right here is Louisville, not St. Louis. Kentucky, not Missouri. She still has a considerable distance to go.

She says that there has been some mistake, that this has been her destination all along, but he is resolute about such matters on account of an absolute faith in the infallibility of the railroad. Instead of fetching her bag, he presses the receipt back into her hand.

She glances up at the window of the car, where Julia's eyes are still shut. At this moment she would do anything but cause a fuss. The price could be entirely too high. It would be far easier to leave her few belongings behind. "I may have given you the wrong receipt," she says, rummaging in the pocket of her apron for the fistful belonging to Julia. "Do you think it might be one of these?"

Confounded, the porter begins to study them one by one.

While he concentrates, Jule steps away and vanishes into the crowds yet milling on the platform. The track runs east to west; this she knows. To the south is trouble. To the north, just across the river, is Indiana. There will be colored men working along the riverbank, sympathetic men who will surely help her cross to safety.

She wrings her empty hands as she slips away. She would say her goodbyes if she could. She would offer a prayer regarding Master Fred's typhoid. She would explain herself as if any explanation might possibly be required.

But no. She must condemn such habituated thoughts to the past. She must vanish unseen into an unknown territory and an unknowable future. In her chest she feels an unaccustomed pang—something to do with the closing of one door and the opening of another—but she does not permit it to last.

He awakens beneath his blanket strangling for air, and he casts it aside, and he goes on strangling still. Although the invader in his throat is a part of him now, a constant thing on par with a knuckle or a tooth, he is far from accustomed to it.

For just this moment—in between sleeping and rising, at the juncture of heart and mind, in the space between train station and mountainside cottage—all such familiar torments become one. His poisonous interloper and Jule's long-endured enchainment and the persistent American rift. People—individuals and races and whole nations—can endure much, but never without consequence. His torment will take his life. Jule's will warp her future beyond reckoning. As for the nation, he has given up considering its fate. What remains now is the work before him. He must finish it, lest his own failings steal the nourishment from his children's very mouths.

CHAPTER 8

1865

The Package—Part Two

The Confederates are in disarray, weakened and half-starved and scattering like so many droplets of mercury, but they are not to be counted out. They could easily go to ground in small groups, making themselves a lasting pestilence upon the countryside. How very like the Confederacy such a tactic would be, in fact. To end the war by not ending it. To take up, at this extreme, the tactics with which Quantrill and his bloody raiders had terrorized the frontier from the beginning. Even now, here in the first week of April, his armies are hastening the process of the Confederates' eventual atomization, slaying hundreds of men and taking dozens more prisoner and separating those who remain into ever smaller bands of ever more vengeful killers. It is a risky business. He must force a surrender, or he shall be compelled to slay them all.

As the Confederate army shrinks in the field, the nation to be restored looms ever larger in his mind. He has thought of nothing but the war for these four years, and now he must think beyond it. The evils of the day about to dawn—acts of violence committed by these men upon their brothers, carried out among these scarred woods and upon these trampled fields and down between the winding sandy banks of these rivers and runs—will live on past today and must be accounted for.

He calls his secretary, Parker, to his field headquarters. Lieutenant Colonel Ely Parker, of the Seneca Nation. The man possesses a deep knowledge of the rules of war and a fine way with the English language and many other skills besides. As an engineer, he was leveraged into the army by Grant himself despite his citizenship or lack thereof. He is a lawyer, too—in every respect but the license, having been denied certification by the state of New York on account of his birth. Together, he and the general draft terms of surrender for Lee's army. The aide who accepts it knows exactly where it must go, for the enemy is only a few miles distant.

———

West to Lynchburg. Lynchburg is the key. Rest and resupply there, and then onward to North Carolina. In North Carolina they can regroup. Make a proper army of themselves again, on home ground.

Grant's letter finds Lee because a blindfolded man could find him.

The contents are simple and clear and completely unacceptable. The terms are all wrong. He would agree to a cessation of hostilities, to a truce between two armies, but not to a surrender. Never to a surrender. He drafts a reply to that effect, although he hates having to spare a man to carry it.

That man, as it turns out, will have a better day than most of the soldiers under Lee's command. He is heading east, after all, east and away from the fighting. A full quarter of the men left to Lee, a handful of his generals included, will be dead by suppertime. The treachery of two exposed and untraversable bridges will be their undoing. The bridges and the Yankees, that is. The bridges and the Yankees and that damned devilish Grant, pressing for a surrender that remains out of the question.

By the last light of day he fetches the package from his trunk. Its swaddling cloths stink a trifle less now or else his environs stink more; it is impossible to say for certain. He cuts the rope from curiosity and unfolds the canvas but goes no further than that. There is more wrapping beneath it, he sees, a sturdy layer of butcher paper bound with string, and he decides that there might be secrets and revelations remaining in this life still.

Along about midnight, a second letter arrives from Grant. Lee tears it open and reads it by candlelight, his hand shaking with fury. The man is incorrigible. He calls once again for surrender, and this time he dares to suggest that from this moment forward any additional blood to be shed—*any further effusion of blood*, he writes, like the veriest poet—will cling exclusively to Lee's hands. He states it as if he himself has no role in this filthy business.

It is the purest cast-iron arrogance.

But let Grant think what he likes. The Army of Northern Virginia will strike him a fresh blow in the morning, and never mind the cost.

————————

Does Lee have such low regard for his men that he will force them through another day of this hopeless, grinding misery? Apparently, for there is no letter of agreement awaiting the general when he rises in the morning. All night long he has lain with one eye open in expectation, and he awakens now with a sick headache to show for it. God bless those Rebel boys. They are far better men than their officers. He cannot say why every single one of them hasn't deserted by now.

When this war is over, he will rejoice to welcome such men as his comrades. An army of them could conquer the world.

Everything is winding down. Today's fighting has a listless brutality about it. Men kill and men die but it is all by rote. There is little apparent point to anything—just movement for its own sake and cruelty out of habit.

The Union claims twenty-five Confederate cannons in the morning's action, along with the contents of a supply train that might have turned the tide. At noon or thereabouts a pair of Confederate wagon trains similarly laden fall the same way. They'd been bound for Appomattox Courthouse, carrying a dream of resupply and revival.

Lee's army straggles into the village in the late afternoon, and they find it a good deal short of the Promised Land.

Once he has attained the privacy of his tent, he sits upon his cot and clips the binding string to free the butcher paper enclosing the package he has been carrying across Virginia from one calamity to the next. He shall see at last what there is to see. He shall learn just how much elegance and grace he will possess at the moment of his disgrace.

The tissue paper beneath, however, gives him pause. It is too pristine to be marred with these terrible unwashed hands of his, to say nothing of the unsullied uniform within. He must go no further now. He must have faith and wait until the last moment.

Grant has another sick headache upon rising, unless it is the same one.

He has slept poorly but his men have slept worse, masses of them marching all night to close in upon the Confederates with the first bloom of the morning. Among them are four thousand members of the United States Colored Troops, four thousand and more, come to play their part in exacting the Union's justice.

———

It is over. There shall be no sudden escape, no miraculous resupply, no brilliant maneuvering, no further action of any sort. He takes up his pen and composes a letter to Grant, requesting a meeting at which they might discuss terms. According to the latest intelligence, he could nail it to a tree a few miles to the east of his tent, and Grant himself would likely come upon it soon enough. He is on his way, and only by riding at the cautionless speed of the Pony Express can messengers from both sides transmit the generals' correspondence back and forth in time.

Grant agrees and asks Lee to name the spot.

Lee does not care a fig about the spot. He consults with his lieutenants and names a nearby farmhouse whose owner is not merely amenable but actually present to give his permission. Most of the village is deserted, and he would hate to trespass.

He polishes his boots with his own two hands and he polishes his dress sword the same. If Grant objects to his arriving so armed, it will be just one more disagreement to be settled, and a small one at that. A petty one compared to the fates of two nations.

He calls for a jug of water and a bit of lye soap and he performs his ablutions, paying special attention to his beard and face and hands. The water is cold and mineral, and it smells of the spawning of fish. He thinks as he splashes himself with it that he shall never do exactly this again. Tomorrow, everything will have changed.

When he is clean, he unwraps the uniform, and he finds it a wonder. It is just the thing for a gentleman to wear when taken prisoner.

His tailor's initials are stitched subtly inside, right in the usual spot. There is comfort in that. It is like a coded message from a reassuring past. He finds everything a trifle loose around the belly, however—the trousers and the waistcoat and the frock coat, too—and he is saddened to think that the quality of the man's work has fallen off. Not until he returns home and sees himself fresh in the hall mirror will he learn how the war has reduced him.

———

Grant arrives at the farmhouse a bit later than Lee, and because it is too painful to talk about this war, they talk about the old war in Mexico. They met briefly in that long-ago action, a pair of soldiers on the march from Vera Cruz. Grant himself looks as if he could have come directly from that assignment to this one, so shabby is his blouse and so muddy are his trousers. He is dressed in the borrowed clothing of an ordinary soldier, with only certain patches and markings haphazardly in place to suggest his rank. He does not require them. Anyone could see that he is the authority at these proceedings.

He settles into a padded swivel chair by a little writing table and nods to Lee that he ought to take an elegant cane chair a few feet distant. It suits his fine uniform better. They settle and talk some more. West Point and the weather. Shared acquaintances. Grant is patient. One particular word will begin this enterprise in earnest, one word of great potency, and he waits for Lee to use it first. Eventually he does.

The general stiffens his back, glances at his lieutenants, and says, "*The surrender of my army*—on what terms will you receive it?"

Surrender. As far as Grant is concerned, Lee has committed enough just by saying it. What gets written down can only be superfluous now, and, as intended, he will keep it to the minimum—for the sake of everyone's dignity. It shall be a modest gentlemen's agreement guaranteeing that no further harm or dishonor comes to these men—or to the one nation that they shall serve going forward. He signals to his secretary, the Iroquois Parker, who comes to his side and sets out a handwritten paper or two.

An ironic twinkle gleams in Lee's eye, and he catches Parker's attention. "I am glad to see one *real* American here," he says, rising and thrusting out his hand.

"We are all Americans," grants the secretary. "And we share a single cause."

Grant beams. The man is irreplaceable. He clears his throat and takes a quick glance at the papers before him. "Our terms are simple," he says. "We require that you lay down your arms, return to your homes, and never again take up action against the government of the United States of America. That is all."

Lee swallows. Whatever he has been expecting in the way of retaliation or even simple justice—trials and tribunals, divestitures and sacrifices, incarcerations and executions—has not materialized. These warring armies are to be enemies no longer and countrymen once again, on the instant. He sighs, and looks Grant squarely in the eye, and quotes the book of John. "'Go, and sin no more'?"

"Exactly," says Grant. "'Go, *and sin no more.*' We shall bind up the nation's wounds and make ourselves once more into the countrymen we have been from the start."

Lee does not know how much he ought to press his good luck, but he gathers his wits and resolves to introduce a condition or two. His men, he says, have been on short rations. Grant agrees that they shall be fed with an open hand. Most of them, he says, have brought their own horses to the front and will require them when they begin to work their farms again. Grant releases the lot. The final condition he does not even need to say out loud; he merely touches the scabbard at his hip with an idle finger, and Grant understands. "Your officers may retain their weapons and their mounts," he says, "and go in peace."

Parker writes everything out, and the generals sign.

It is all over but the fusillades of celebratory gunfire, which will travel outward from this spot in echoing circles as unit after unit receives the news of this most gracious of reconciliations, this rarest of kindnesses, this gift without attachment.

The tailor's bill goes unpaid and unacknowledged, and so it shall be until the end of time. Complaint is as impossible as it is useless. The chain of command lies broken in the ashes of history. The better part of Richmond is in ruins. The taverns where so much business was conducted are ghost houses now, if they stand at all. And the headquarters of the army, once a hive of concentrated activity, stands blackened, hollowed out, empty as an upright grave. Jefferson Davis has vamoosed to parts unknown.

His own shop still stands, for reasons knowable only to God.

The tailor takes down the remnant of gray English wool from its spot on the highest shelf, wondering if his imagination has somehow warped his understanding of the affair. Perhaps he has allowed the matter of Lee's last uniform to grow outsized and over-important in his mind. His passion has made it grandiose. Very well, then. He shall see the truth for himself. He half expects to find within the box an unassuming length of humble gray serge, stuff suited to the hard use of debasement.

He slits the paper strip and opens the lid and is relieved to discover that his enthusiasm has not deceived him. The remnant is as he remembers it, a small piece of perfection, untouched and inviolate.

He nods to himself and closes the box again, not sealing it as he did before but tearing the paper strip clean off all the way around. There is no use in making a reliquary of it. Let the moths have it if they will.

Forty Days and Forty Nights

Sam Willett buys passage on the train from Albany, paying out of his own pocket. It is the least he can do. The old fellow is slim and erect as a cattail stalk, and he wears for the duty his old uniform from the Grand Army of the Republic. It still fits well enough. He has pressed it himself and mended a tear or two in the seams and patched a dozen holes that moths have eaten through the fabric despite his keeping it in a cedar chest with pungent cakes of naphthalene.

He and Grant are about the same age, but thanks to a life of better fortune—not counting the passing this year of his wife, Clara—he bears the decades with more grace. Willett is one of the few lucky soldiers who came through the war without some wound to body or mind. They are a rare and privileged brotherhood of utter strangers. Were you to ask one, he would tell you that the chance of meeting a single further example of his kind is that of encountering an archangel on horseback.

He has with him a steamer trunk and a big leather satchel and a canvas backpack. He needs a little assistance to get the whole business assembled and in motion, but once he is under way—backpack over his shoulders, satchel in his fist, one edge of the steamer trunk scraping roughly over the ground—he is confident that he could walk five or even ten miles. It would not be much compared to the vast distances he once covered on foot for the 3rd New York, but for a man of his age it is a source of pride.

Outside the train station in Saratoga Springs he makes for a curious sight, a dignified throwback to an era long past, the sort of old-timer you might see bearing the colors in an Independence Day parade. He gains the attention of a young farmer passing by with a wagonload of supplies and persuades him that making a side trip to Mount McGregor is in his best interest. It costs a fair portion of the money remaining in his wallet, but no matter. He climbs aboard the wagon bed and makes himself passably comfortable on the steamer trunk, but the young farmer won't have it. The old soldier seems to him marked in some way, more worthy than the run of ordinary men, deserving of special treatment. He invites him up to share his seat on the box, and off they go.

After a little while, the young man says, "The president is up there, you know."

"The president? He'll always be the general to me."

"On Mount McGregor, I mean. Staying in somebody's cottage or other."

"I know it. That's why I'm going."

"You and everybody else."

"That's another reason."

A vacant look from the young man.

"All those folks crowding around, somebody needs to take guard duty."

Sure enough, his baggage contains all the necessities for an encampment, including a regulation six-man pup tent complete with stakes and ropes, a folding chair, a hatchet, a file and a whetstone and a little vial of oil, a crosscut saw, a frying pan and a Dutch oven, a coffeepot, soap in bars and powdered, eating utensils, a tin plate and cup, a clasp knife and other small implements, reading material to last a month, an American flag, a short-handled shovel, matches and candles and a kerosene lamp, two changes of clothing, tinned oysters and canned beans and a quantity of hardtack, a rope cot, a white cotton night-shirt and a pair of red long johns with a trapdoor in the back, shoe polish, writing implements and a supply of stationery, assorted rags and brushes, a rolled-up towel, and two thick blankets of heavy green wool. He shall fashion tent poles and a flagpole and a frame for the cot from deadfalls, and a platform from split logs should a platform be required. At the bottom of his backpack is a little-used harmonica that he has brought on a whim, mainly for the sake of campfire custom. He cannot play much beyond "Yankee Doodle" and "My Old Kentucky Home," and only the first seems appropriate for the circumstances, but tradition is tradition.

He drops his things alongside the trail and reports immediately to the cottage, only to find Grant asleep on the porch beneath a rumpled mess of blankets. This he takes as a bad sign. He knocks softly on the door and is quietly admitted by Harrison Terrell. In the kitchen he introduces himself to Julia and Fred and provides his credentials and outlines his intentions. Seeing no harm in it and perhaps a little benefit, they let him set up camp just a little way down the mountain-side, in a flat spot alongside the pathway. There he shall intercept would-be visitors, assess their intentions, and decide whether or not to let them pass.

Julia stipulates that he may not possess a weapon while on duty, which suits him fine because he has brought nothing more usefully menacing than the clasp knife. In time she will provide him with a list of individuals to be admitted directly, and a shorter list of those to be turned away as coolly as he finds decent. For now he must use his own judgment on such matters. At the very least he is to keep out curiosity seekers and those drawn here by impending tragedy.

Setting up camp is not so easy or automatic as it was when he served in the 3rd New York. He is alone now, supplied with the usual number of arms and hands, and stymied at every turn by a tent made in two separate halves so as to be carried and erected by two men. He is lucky to get the confounded thing up and his possessions moved inside before a storm comes rolling up the mountain from out of the west. It brings a downpour, a cold and steady summer rain with traces of winter still in it. He sits dutifully on the folding chair with a blanket clutched around his shoulders, watching the wind lash the treetops and wishing he'd had time to lay in a supply of firewood.

CHAPTER 9

1867

Dent

He is not without detractors, both public and personal. Chief among them is Colonel Dent, who would disown him if only they had an actual blood relation that he might sever. He has reasons galore for feeling this way. By his lights, his son-in-law possesses the table manners of a peasant, comports himself too rambunctiously with the children, dotes too openly upon his wife, drinks to excess, eats to excess, smokes to excess, speaks too freely, wears his hat wrong, rides a horse too carelessly, associates with too many men of questionable reputation, has too many friends in excessively high places, pays too much for everything, swings a scythe with less caution than common sense would advise, treats hired people of all colors too kindly, wouldn't know a good coon dog if it bit him, and possesses too high an opinion of himself.

"There shall always be a place at my table for Julia," he tells the preacher one Sunday morning, "but none for that husband of hers."

"I doubt he'll go hungry," says the preacher, pumping Dent's right hand. "You might be the only man in America who'd refuse him a plate."

"Oh, he'll take a handout, he will. There's no question about that."

The preacher smiles. "And don't forget his military pay."

"For which he does as little as possible. *Commanding General of the Armies*, they call him. We've gotten along without one of those since Washington gave up the job. Someday the nation will come to its senses and cut him clean off."

"He'd keep his pension, of course."

"His pension, yes. He's a great one to take something for nothing."

"Now, now," says the preacher. "He earned it. Let us be charitable."

"He doesn't deserve charity. Not yours and not mine and certainly not the government's."

The preacher smiles a pained smile and releases the colonel's hand. If it weren't for his faith in the power of redemption, he would give the fellow up for a poor investment.

Between trips to Washington and the demands of his father-in-law's farm, Grant barely has time to be a proper husband these days, never mind a father. You would think that the hero of Chattanooga would be the master of some aspect of his own life, but he is not. The army goes its peacetime way with or without his counsel. White Haven demands of him a farm's ordinary exhausting excess, especially now that Dent's slaves have been freed to seek their poor fortunes elsewhere. He hardly sees Julia and the children. Most of his daily transactions involve hired men or gentlemen of commerce or the bitter old colonel himself, and there is no question as to which of these he tolerates with the least enthusiasm.

The newspaper reports plague him as well, and lacking the time to read them is a blessing. News penetrates his consciousness nonetheless. It arrives directly from Washington via mail and telegram and messenger, and in every dispatch he finds new evidence that the war is not entirely over. Hostilities go on unabated—not so much between the North and the South as between the principles that continue to guide them along their different paths.

It is a war undeclared but nonetheless fought, day by dispiriting day.

The slave population has been freed but is by no means free. Its individual members are bound by chains of economic servitude and cultural loathing, and every single government policy established to lift them up is either ignored or subverted outright. In county after Southern county, lone black men and boys, most of them guilty of little more than drawing breath, are terrorized and pursued and viciously murdered by gangs of the very same individuals who once were satisfied to own them body and soul. The killers gouge out their eyes and tear out their tongues and hack away their reproductive organs in fits of gleeful destruction. They hang them from cottonwoods and great live oaks like bled livestock, like tanned hides, like the spoils of some savage conquest.

He reads the dispatches from Washington and shakes his head and sighs. Some days he concludes that the war was either a failure or something much worse: a sham, a charade, a cynical confidence game whose object was to weaken the powers of good and set hell's every last demon free. He himself was surely taken in by the seductive optimism of its promises. He can remember believing that to settle the war would be to reunite the nation, as if peace itself had some power to command men's hearts. As if slogging through the killing fields of Gettysburg or Antietam or Shiloh would somehow set an individual—set an entire nation, in fact—on a permanent course of unbending virtue.

It was not to be. The conclusion rattles him, threatening to take away whatever self-built framework keeps him upright from one day to the next. He says so to Julia one night as he puts out the lamp. "What do you think might have happened," he asks, his voice emerging from blackness as the flame chokes and dies, "if I had been less forgiving of Lee?"

"At Appomattox?"

"At Appomattox."

"I don't know that you *forgave* him, exactly."

"But I did place my trust in him. I placed my trust in every single one of those men." A little fog of moonlight has begun to peep through the window and his eyes have adjusted to the darkness and he watches the shape of her as she moves in the bed, a shadow among greater shadows.

"You did what Lincoln wanted you to do."

He shakes his head, although she does not make it out. "I followed my instincts."

"Your instincts aligned with his."

"Fair enough. Then let us agree that both Lincoln and I let them off too lightly. That does not excuse my lenience. I am as much at fault as he is. More so, for he was not present at the transaction, and I oversaw it."

"Your orders were clear."

"I could have bent them a trifle."

"If you had, you wouldn't be the man I love."

"My sympathies were not those of a victor but those of a soldier. They ran along with those of other soldiers, even my sworn enemies."

"I'm not surprised. I know you."

"By God, Julia, Lee arrived as if he were dressed for a state dinner, even though he surely expected to be taken to prison. It preserved his dignity, I think. How could I fail to be touched by such a thing?"

"It spoke to your better nature."

"It weakened me—so much that I sent them all home. I told myself that they had seen the light."

"Some did. More will."

"And what of my poor dead soldiers? What of those boys who gave up their lives pursuing a victory that I was too weak to chase all the way to the ground? I swear to you, Julia, they died for my sins."

Dent's health declines, and he spends most of his days in bed. Grant rejoices at his absence—the youngest of Julia's brothers, Louis, takes over for him and proves a far more amenable working partner—but he does not let his delight show, leastwise around her. Even the most disagreeable of family is still family.

Dent blames his troubles, both medical and financial, on the war and its resolution. In this he is not entirely wrong. White Haven was built upon a dream, after all—a dream of white abundance and black privation, of white triumph and black ruin. The dream served him well for years, and he has not yet fully awoken from it. If he does, he will arise into a different dream altogether, this one a vision of the ruined past as some glorious Edenic enterprise now crushed beneath a foreign heel.

The tatters of this vision persist as well in the minds of the many brutal men who haunt the dark, lonesome byways of the sweet sunny South.

They call themselves the Klan and they are organized the way a hurricane is organized, madly a-spin around a terrible void. That void is hatred, and it draws every weak and broken thing to it. In truth, the group's members belong to nothing that can be seen or identified, and they are fated to know each other chiefly by their works. They share deep memories, none of them genuine, of a romantic past swept clean of labor and want. Often they unconsciously adopt formations that mimic the structure of the vanquished army for which they once bled, hobbling old veterans and merciless young men alike reporting once more to their former officers, all of them draped now in home-sewn garments of white, white, white.

Old Dent does not rejoice in reports of their far-ranging and random vengeance, because he has reached the point in his descent where he rejoices in nothing. Not even in Julia. She brings him special pain, in fact, for he cannot think of her without thinking of how carelessly she has thrown away her life on Grant. Without Grant and his scheming and his high-minded deceit, the Confederacy would have triumphed, and White Haven would remain as it once was, and Julia would be in line to be the empress of it. Her own husband has undermined and stolen her patrimony and left them all the poorer for it. On this account the man's praises are sung from sea to shining sea.

So it is that he is resolutely unimpressed when she brings good news to him upon his bed of pain. The Radical Republicans in Washington have persuaded her husband to run for the presidency.

"Oh, marvelous," says Dent.

There has been a great national crying out for his candidacy.

"Most excellent," says Dent.

His victory will be all but certain.

"Wonderful," says Dent. And before Julia can go on, he draws the deepest breath he can and fires his one and only shell: "And how shall he earn his living, once this pipe dream is ended?"

"Why, he shall have his military pension."

Dent barks out a laugh that costs him dearly. Once he has collected himself—with the help of Julia's slapping him on the back a half dozen times and dabbing away at his wet lips with a corner of the bedsheet—he squeaks out an answer. "They don't let generals run things in Washington no matter how great their momentary celebrity."

Julia does not miss the implication. "'Momentary celebrity'?"

"These things pass, as a rule. Besides, he shall be required to surrender his commission when he takes up the office. And with it will go his claim on a pension."

"That's impossible."

"It is not. It's the truth."

Julia bites at her lip for a moment. "What do other presidents do when they no longer serve?"

"They're usually wealthy to begin with. If not, they live off the kindness of men for whom they have done favors while in office. Secret favors."

"Father," she says, aghast, "that would never be the case. You know Ulysses."

"I know him well. He's so upright, he'll starve to death—and take you with him."

"Then we'll return here. We'll always have Hardscrabble."

"Hardscrabble wouldn't support a family of mice. And I won't have him working at White Haven again, either." He adds a little theatrical cough to drive home his point, and it becomes a real cough soon enough, and Julia waits for it to subside on its own.

In a few months' time, the old colonel will endure a punishing stroke, and Ulysses will step back to prepare for what looks certain to be the presidency, and Louis will take over the management of White Haven altogether. The fragile old colonel who is not a colonel, confined to his bed, will eventually be moved to a private suite in the White House. There he shall live out his remaining years in the undeserved and underappreciated comfort that he believes to be his due.

Forty Days and Forty Nights

The grandchildren adopt him first. Little Julia and Ulysses, up from New York to rusticate while their grandfather wages his last campaign. They have the run of the place, as they should. Imagine their delight when they discover a kindly old soldier encamped only a few dozen yards from their front door. They have seen his kind a hundred times, subdued and gracious supplicants come to pay their respects to their grandfather. They have witnessed public halls and city streets crowded with them. They have seen them marching in formation, making up entire parades. They know that they have nothing to fear from the likes of these, and when they catch sight of the old fellow at work in the woods, they run to his side.

At the moment, Sam Willett is busy repairing the damage caused by last night's rainstorm. Having lacked the time to establish camp properly, he neglected to dig a trench around his tent. He regrets it now. Rivulets of streaming water have cut channels into the earth where the tent stood, saturating his belongings from the ground up. He digs a trench now and he shall build a platform by and by. In the meantime, he has hung his clothing and linens from the lowest branches of the trees roundabout, and their haphazard arrangement gives his little claim the shabby but gay air of a bazaar in some exotic locale.

The children begin an impromptu game behind and around and beneath the articles hung out to dry, a high-spirited mix of Ghost in the Graveyard and Capture the Flag and some other game whose rules are known to no other children on earth. They shriek with joy and whoop with delight, and Willett—here to do his bit for their paterfamilias in his last days—finds it all comforting. *Life will go on*, he thinks. So it will. Yet he must serve the general while he can.

The sounds of the children at play bring Grant to the window, and from there to the porch. He moves at a glacial pace, his cane stumping and his slippered feet shuffling on the floorboards. He wears long, loose pajamas and has a black blanket gathered around his neck, partly concealing the swelling of the tumor that blooms ever larger in his throat. He is so changed, so reduced, that Willett would hardly know him on sight, and yet there could be no mistaking him for any other man. He has a gravity about him, an unmistakable and overwhelming power that belies his decay. Willett leans toward the cottage as if drawn by a lodestone, and he looks up toward his figure as he would have looked at a certain gentleman delivering the Sermon on the Mount.

Grant clears his throat as best he can.

Willett drops his shovel and throws back his shoulders and snaps off a salute so brisk and angular that you'd swear he's been practicing it all week, which is indeed the case. "General, sir," he says. "At your service, sir."

Grant smiles, beatific. "Mrs. Grant tells me you've volunteered for guard duty." His voice is so soft and low that listening to it draws Willett forward against his will.

"Yes, sir. I have, sir."

"She also advises me that breakfast is ready, if you would be so kind as to join us at the table." The general turns back toward the house, takes a heavy step or two, and pauses to endure a protracted fit of coughing. He leans heavily upon his cane, his body bent.

Sam Willett half wishes that he hadn't been invited in, but there is no avoiding it now. Caught with his hands begrimed and his boots caked with mud, he takes a few tentative steps toward the cottage and calls out an offer of assistance to the general. His voice emerges in a kind of ragged falsetto, a mingling of panic and awe.

Grant takes one hand away from the cane just long enough to wave him off. He does not turn his head to make eye contact—at this stage of the disease he cannot twist his neck more than five or ten degrees without bringing on excruciating pain—but Willett gets his meaning. He would help any other man so broken, but in this case he shall wait for Grant to make his own slow passage and then, after a decent interval, follow him in.

Soon enough, the children abandon their game and come running to escort Willett up the porch steps. Their buoyancy lifts him up and carries him inside, where they all remove their muddy shoes under Julia's imperious eye. Once in the dining room, he finds Grant at the table in a wheeled chair. The family eats in shifts, it seems, for the only other adults present are Julia and Nellie. He bows to each of them, protests that they must not make any fuss on his behalf, and asks if he might please be excused to wash his hands before sitting down.

Breakfast is eggs and bacon and hotcakes, every bite steaming fresh from the kitchen. Willett confesses that he's expected such folks as the Grants to dine on meals brought down from the hotel, but Julia scoffs and says she's gotten used to cooking for a big family again, ever since . . . well . . . A sorrowful look from the general discourages her. The children eat like racehorses—well-mannered racehorses, but racehorses all the same, especially little Ulysses, who would seem to be filling up a hollow leg—sending their aunt Nellie back and forth to the kitchen after seconds and thirds. The general speaks only a little and takes nothing but coffee, black, which he drinks sip by cautious sip. Apparently he is here not for nourishment but for the pleasure of spending a few moments with the children. He has so much to do, and so little time in which to do it.

Willett never again sets foot in the cottage but remains at his post day and night. He learns the schedule of the train in the valley by listening for its whistle and assessing foot traffic along the pathway. There is usually a pulse of visitors at ten in the morning, another just after noon, and one more around two thirty. There are exceptions, of course—stragglers and strangers and solitary travelers of questionable intent—but although he keeps an eye out for them, his days mostly rise and fall with the rhythm of the railroad.

Some visitors make the journey more than once, and he comes to recognize them and even strike up a little conversation from time to time. There is the famous author Mr. Clemens, who seems enchanted with the sound of his own voice. There is a Methodist bishop from New York, the unctuous John Philip Newman, who seems chiefly interested in applying the balm of religion to the soul of Mrs. Grant, never mind her husband. And there is the inestimable General William Tecumseh Sherman, whom Willett identifies at a glance from his military posture, his short-clipped beard, and his penetrating glare. These and a few others he summons to the head of the line that they might not have to linger behind other, lesser visitors, but only Clemens and the bishop accept.

He admits callers from Julia's list of approved individuals—various politicians both retired and active, the editor of Grant's magazine pieces, a financier or two—and he assesses the remainder on terms that he refines as he goes along. It proves easy enough to identify those who desire nothing more than to witness the spectacle of a great man brought low. He can tell them by the look in their eyes, by the cut of their clothing, by their unseemly good cheer. Some are too young to have followed the general's triumphs in the newspapers, and for these he has the natural pity that age has for inexperience. Others seem peculiar at best and dangerous at worst, strange in manner and shifty of eye. Some have the look of men with a bone to pick. Regardless of the particulars, he finds a certain satisfaction in sending them all packing. The general's work must go on.

At Mrs. Grant's request, he gives special consideration to old soldiers. Union or Confederate, it matters not. Her husband loves them all the same. He cannot help himself.

CHAPTER 10

1875

Santo Domingo

The president has come for counsel but he does not go directly to the subject of interest, for a more immediate matter has intervened.

"Where is your usual man today?" he asks.

"Terrell?"

"I hope he hasn't taken a position elsewhere." Grant can hardly imagine this great house—the residence of Washington's most eminent banker, his friend George Washington Riggs—without Terrell to greet him at the door.

"Oh, no, Mr. President. I would be very reluctant to part with him."

Grant smiles, relieved. "I have little doubt."

"There isn't enough money in the world," says Riggs, lifting his palm to indicate the room and the house and the whole luxurious universe that lies here under his ownership. By the look of things, he has already spent half the money in the world, and he is keeping the other half for an emergency.

Grant laughs.

A girl enters bearing a tray with tea for the banker and coffee for the president. Riggs addresses her. "Mr. Terrell has the day off, is that correct?"

"Oh, yes, sir. Yes, he does."

"He'll be seeing off that no-account son of his. Isn't that right?"

The girl crumples with laughter barely contained. "I should say. '*That no-account son of his.*'"

Riggs explains quickly, lest there be any doubt in the president's mind. "Young Terrell is bound for Groton, you see."

Dumbfounded, Grant lifts his coffee cup and blows across its surface for a moment, considering. "Groton? Very impressive."

"As is the young man himself."

Grant leans in with the air of a conspirator. "Of course, it doesn't hurt to have friends in high places."

"I wouldn't know," says Riggs.

Grant lights a cigar and they turn to the matter at hand. "Santo Domingo," he says. "Where do you stand on the proposal?"

"I am dead set against it."

Grant looks puzzled.

"Annexing the place would benefit some, I suppose. Mainly the individuals who cooked up the idea."

"Fabens?"

"Fabens. He and his friend, that Cazneau. Two greater villains never lived."

"Fabens is a businessman."

"And Cazneau is a general. To my knowledge, neither position has ever marked a man for sainthood."

"I suppose not."

"Just between the two of us, Mr. President, they've been investing there for years. They own a good deal of the country by now."

"No."

"And they haven't wasted a penny. Everything has gone into timber, mining, shipping . . ."

"How have I not heard about this?"

"You're hearing now. I've never handled financing for those two, but I know full well who does."

Grant draws on his cigar. "Very well, then," he says, "but what about the colored? Where are they to go if we don't let them have Santo Domingo?"

"They ought to stay right here at home."

Grant clucks. "Santo Domingo would make a marvelous refuge."

"They ought not to require a refuge."

"Their troubles are very great just now. So great that they infect the entire nation."

"We ought not to resolve it by sending them into exile."

Grant bridles. "We wouldn't *send* anyone. Families could relocate if they desired."

"I still oppose it." He counts the reasons out on his fingers: "First, we ought to be able to solve our own problems. Second, Fabens and Cazneau must not be rewarded for their mendacity. Third, if their scheme should come out in the end, people might get the impression that you were complicit."

"I have no concern for my reputation," says Grant. "I don't plan on seeking a higher office when I'm finished with this one. I'll need no references."

The banker shrugs. "Very well, Mr. President. You have heard my counsel."

"I'll give it thought."

"Do. People shouldn't be running off to Santo Domingo. They should be encouraged to stay home and aim higher. Not everyone can be our young Robert Terrell, but there are possibilities everywhere."

Forty Days and Forty Nights

Young Ulysses has a harmonica, too, as it happens, and although he can't play it, his sister, Julia, can. At least a little. She and Willett agree to collaborate—between pulses of visitors from the valley train—on an arrangement of that old favorite, "Oh! Susanna." They get it very nearly right. She knows the words to the first two verses cold and he knows the words to another verse in a general way, and so after they've played it through enough times they take turns singing. Willett has a voice like a bullfrog and Julia's could be mistaken for a wood thrush, and they make a marvelously unlikely pair. Clemens, who pauses to listen one afternoon as he makes his way down the hill, remarks that they suggest to him an old cowpoke and his little pardner, crouched around a campfire on the high plains.

Young Ulysses can always be counted upon to applaud every performance as if he's never heard music played better. It's likely that he has not. Julia generally stands to curtsey when they're finished, but Willett stays seated rather than wear out his knees.

Willett resists when Julia suggests they stage a recital for her grandfather. Oh, he says, we dare not call him away from his work. The general is a busy, busy man. He means this, as far as it goes, but there is another explanation. A deeper one. From across the breakfast table on that very first morning, he saw that Grant would rather be with his grandchildren than anywhere else, and he suspects it would be the height of cruelty to demonstrate how much time he has been spending with them in the general's stead.

So it is out of decency that their musical efforts remain confined to the little clearing in the woods below the cottage—in the privacy of the tent, if Willett can arrange it. The general, imprisoned in his rooms and sometimes in his very bed, is thus either spared or deprived of their music.

In dreams both waking and sleeping he is caught up in the siege of Petersburg. Every step he takes there is a step in the wrong direction, every strategy he works out comes to nothing, and there would seem to be no end in sight. Even getting this passage on paper is taking longer than should be necessary. He fears that he may shuffle off this mortal life before the work is done.

He has gotten as far as the Battle of the Crater, or at least its beginnings. One of his lieutenants, a mining engineer from the mountains of Pennsylvania by the name of Pleasants, has proposed a strategy so improbable that only a man desperate or mad would consider it. He advises that they disrupt the rail interchange at Petersburg by digging a long tunnel to a location directly beneath one of its key crossings, planting a great volume of explosives, and blowing the entire business to kingdom come.

"It worked well enough in Vicksburg," he says, and Grant cannot say otherwise.

Believing the project will have the added benefit of keeping the men busy, he authorizes it. Morale has no enemy more dangerous and cunning than idleness, and idleness has been the order of the day for too long. Pleasants and a party of his engineers choose a spot for digging and plot out a course as accurately as the limitations of distance and access permit. The digging starts on a rainy Virginia morning, when at Pleasants's order the men set upon the very earth beneath their feet. They throw themselves into the work, toiling away with the satisfaction and glee of demons digging themselves a passage back to hell. The work is exhausting, and they can measure their progress by little more than an inch at a time, but before a week has passed, the diggers at the face are underground and out of sight. They labor by torchlight, and a second crew is brought in to build a ventilation system of Pleasants's design, without which they would all surely suffocate.

Grant receives daily reports but is not much cheered by them. Secretly, he hopes that some tactical miracle will present itself before the tunnel is put to use. He would hate to expend the enormous quantity of gunpowder that will be required, particularly for a result as uncertain as blowing open a crater somewhere in the general vicinity of Petersburg, Virginia.

Tonight he is at his desk while the rest of the encampment sleeps. Only the pickets on duty and a handful of nerveless worriers and a staring drunk or two remain awake to keep him distant company. These few and whatever detail is still laboring away in the tunnel's undifferentiated darkness. As for him, he is strategizing. He is studying maps, analyzing positions, and predicting enemy movements. He is trying out in his mind his own army's possible responses. He is thinking that all of his diligent planning may be thrown into a cocked hat when that damned crater opens up, if it ever does.

The night is dark beneath a clouded moon, and he steps wearily out into it. He ought to go to bed. Any sensible man would. But instead he begins to walk the encampment alone, doing the same work in his head that he has been doing at his desk. He has the maps memorized, after all. They are as fixed in his mind's eye as the framed daguerreotypes that hang over the mantel in his parlor back home. Blinded by darkness, he sees the maps in his mind and he pictures movement upon them in the fields and farms and woodlands surrounding the town. He sees not penciled arrows and scribbled notes and sketched-in details of the countryside but real soldiers moving on a real landscape. Likewise, he feels himself not hovering at some godly or ghostly remove but on foot among them and thus vulnerable to the same fearful risks that assail them daily. Ambushes. Snipers. Unmapped obstacles never seen by scouting parties—rail fences and thick underbrush and narrow, sunken defiles—which restrict movement and create opportunities for disaster.

Enchanted thus, he passes the last ring of tents and their slumbering inhabitants and finds himself nearing the open mouth of the tunnel. He expects to see a light from its depths or at least the hint of a light, but there is none. No sound reaches his ears. It is a puzzle. He wonders how many nights have passed with no detail at work here. Someone needs to be disciplined, most likely. He shall take it up with Pleasants in the morning.

He lingers there for a moment, listening to the light wind in the trees and the steady chirp of insects. When he has been quiet enough for long enough, he hears something else at last: the sound of music. A harmonica, perhaps two of them, and singing too. It is a rough-and-ready version of "Oh! Susanna," the sort of music you might hear around a campfire. "It rained all night the day I left," sings the first voice. It is the voice of a child, perhaps a drummer boy trying out a new instrument. The second voice, when it comes, could not differ more. It is the voice of a man—an old one, to judge by all the signs—and although it is weak in spots and the singer seems a trifle uncertain about the words, it echoes nicely from the tunnel, an octave or maybe even two beneath the other.

He wishes he had a light. A candle would serve, or a lantern, or even a lucifer to ignite one of the torches stacked around the perimeter of the excavation. He steps slowly and cautiously into the tunnel, but he is surprised to note that the music grows no louder as he goes. It is as if the players are moving deeper and deeper at his approach, or as if he is not actually advancing at all. Neither of these conditions is possible, of course. The tunnel is only so long, and he feels its stony surface beneath the soles of his boots as he takes step after cautious step.

Until suddenly a veil is lifted.

Morning comes or at least a hint of it, blazing light filtered mysteriously through the darkness. He seems to find himself existing in both states at once, black night and brilliant day. How odd. How impossible. He groans and reaches out a curious hand . . . and is surprised to hear the light clack of something striking against a wooden floor.

His pencil, dropped.

His extended hand encounters fabric of some sort.

The black blanket, gone over his head while he has slept in the chair.

He shifts the blanket aside and strains to hear the music as if his dream of Petersburg were real. Somewhere, faintly, the two musicians—if musicians they might be called, by any standard—have started over at the beginning. "I come from Alabama, with my banjo on my knee," sings the piping voice of the drummer boy.

But it is no drummer boy. The old general is clearheaded about that now. It is his little Julia, unmistakable. He hears her voice rising from the woods like the voice of an angel. "Be not afraid," it ought to say, instead of "Susanna, don't you cry . . ."

The other voice belongs to Willett.

He throws off the blanket and sets aside the stack of writing paper that materializes in his lap, and then—wincing from the pain in his throat—he calls out for Terrell. "Bring me my cane," he says, "and help me up, if you will be so kind."

Once they have gained the porch, the music is a bit louder, although it is yet filtered by trees. He asks Terrell to go down the hill and bring them back if he may, Julia and Willett, harmonicas and all. His life at this point is all about time and its proper use, but if he has sufficient hours for a nap at midday, he has enough for this.

CHAPTER 11

1882

Vigilance

He is a child of transformation, born into one world and raised up in another. Only six years of age when Lincoln issued the Proclamation. Old enough to remember, too young to have fully understood.

Robert Terrell, born at time's fulcrum.

The general has never once met him face-to-face, although he has heard stories of his achievements. Despite the father's having withheld the son until now, Grant has grown proud of him—proud of Robert and proud of his own personal role in his manufacture. Where would the young man be without Grant, whose army sent the Confederates staggering back home to the reunited United States of America? He would still be on the Virginia plantation where he was born, occupied with God knows what kind of degrading forced labor. His body would be chained to that cursed ground. His soul would never rise above it. And his mind—his fine mind, educated not only at Groton but more recently at Harvard—would languish, untested and unimproved.

The general could go on, and he surely would, were his reverie not interrupted by a knock at the front door. He makes a show of rearranging the papers on his desk as Harrison strides past his study to answer it. Who has come to call? Vanderbilt? Clemens? Perhaps Barnum, in the city to install some new fraud at his museum? He would be happy to visit with any of them.

The air pressure drops with the opening of the front door, and a little gasp emerges from Harrison. "Good Lord," the man says, sounding caught between a terrible beginning and a tragic end, trapped in a present that may not prove as comfortable as he's been given to believe. The door creaks as he begins to push it closed. "You come around back, son," he says. "Around the kitchen door."

"Around the kitchen door?" Robert's voice is deeper than his father's, and it has a Brahmin roundness to it. If he is not yet ready to pass judgment from some elevated judicial bench, he will be ready soon. "It's not as if I'm delivering anything—beyond good wishes, I mean."

"Good wishes come around the back too. Now, go on."

A little crumpled shadow might pass across Robert's face, but it proves to be of no weight.

Harrison leans a shoulder to the door and turns his head, startled by a creaking of the floorboards, to find the general peering from around the corner like an army scout on the perilous edge of unknown territory.

Grant coughs, swallows, wipes his lip with the back of his hand. "Harrison," he asks, "would that be your Robert?"

"Yes, sir." Easing up on the door a little. "Yes, sir—it's my Robert all right."

"Let the man in!"

"Mr. Grant, I was just telling him—"

"I heard. And now I'm telling you."

Harrison dutifully swings wide the door.

Robert smiles a practiced smile and steps inside. "Mr. President," he says, with exactly the correct measure of deference.

A product of West Point with advanced coursework carried out on the battlefield, Grant has always had unsettled ideas about too much education. He thinks of the classroom as a shortcut to adulthood, a substitute for genuine experience. At the same time, he is inclined to envy anyone who has had the opportunity to enjoy so smooth and unquestioned a path. An educated man possesses the future and a diploma to carry into it. A self-made man has only his past, and he must forever be trotting it out for inspection.

In Robert Terrell, however—in his words and in his silences—he detects a refinement both innate and highly polished. Some of it may be his long experience in the classroom, where he has grown accustomed to listening and to giving the impression of listening. He stands engaged and at his ease while they converse a bit, and he attends to Grant's words with little smiles and small wrinkles of agreement and a variety of other subtle indicators that lie likely somewhere between the natural and the cultivated.

Only at a similarly understated message from his father—a shift in stance, a gentle release of breath, surely nothing half so coarse as "It's time we left Mr. Grant to his business"—does Robert begin, subtly but ineluctably, to disengage and move along.

Grant sees it for the refinement it is, and he sees it echoed or perhaps even originating in the older Terrell. How has he overlooked it, or denied it outright, until now? These two men, born with deep resources untapped, born awaiting rescue by the rough barbarians of the U.S. Army. The world seems almost upside down for a moment.

*　　*　　*

In the kitchen, his father takes a step back. "Let me have a good look," he says, and then: "What's wrong, boy?" As if this accomplished grown man is a child again.

"Nothing, Pop."

"Come on. I know better. What ails you?"

Robert shrugs. "I'm not the one ailing."

Harrison clicks his tongue. "Who is it?"

"It's this whole godforsaken world," says Robert.

"Come on, sit down." He ushers his son to the table, places a glass of milk before him, and takes a seat. "Tell me," he says.

"You remember George Wells from back home? Younger than I am by a little?"

"I believe I do."

"He's dead, Pop."

"No."

"A week ago. He died in Maryland."

Harrison reaches a consoling hand to Robert's. "What did him in? Smallpox? Typhus?"

"No."

"Accident?"

Robert shakes his head.

"Must have been drink, then. A world of trouble comes from drink."

Robert lifts his eyes to his father's. "They hanged him, Pop. They hanged him and they shot him with four different guns and they left him swinging from a tree."

"No."

"George was no saint, but he didn't deserve that. Not in a million years."

"I'll be damned. Little George Wells."

"He'd grown up in the meantime."

"Grown up just like you." The look in his father's eyes mingles pride and terror.

"He grew up and moved to Maryland, and this is what it amounted to." He gives his head a rueful shake. "Folks call it lynching, but it's just white men killing black men. It's just another word for how it's always been." He reaches into his pocket and slides a newspaper clipping toward his father.

George Wells, aged 21 years, was hanged in Anne Arundel County by a party of masked men.

Wells had been accused of theft and arrested and duly charged, but his case had never gone to trial. He did not live long enough. He was responsible, everyone knew, for a rash of break-ins around Stony Creek. The robberies were all accomplished with a similar technique and at similar hours of the night, and therefore they all were done by the same man. That man was George Wells. So went the reasoning. Wells himself was noncommittal on the subject when accused from time to time in various parts of the county.

Eventually, men from all around formed a vigilance committee to call at his home at about two o'clock in the morning. Wells answered the door fully dressed, as any nocturnal thief would have been, and the case was settled immediately. One member of the committee fired a shotgun in his direction. Sadly, the fellow was drunk and his aim was off.

The following afternoon Wells was brought to the courthouse for a hearing, and it was there that he committed a crime more grievous than theft. He behaved in a gay and disrespectful manner in the presence of the judge. This violated no particular statute but was nonetheless deemed punishable with all appropriate speed, especially as it had taken place in the presence of a dozen witnesses, some of whom were themselves members of the vigilance committee.

The remainder happened quickly. Wells was charged, and at day's end he was loaded into a wagon under the supervision of two deputies. They set out for the jail in Annapolis, where Wells was to be confined until trial. Shortly after nightfall, their journey was interrupted by a party of masked men who chased off the deputies at gunpoint, escorted Wells into a nearby wooded area, and hanged him from a cottonwood tree. Whether the shots to his body were fired before or after the hanging remains unknown. The coroner judged them of little consequence.

"So you knew the man," says Grant.

"I knew him as a boy," says Robert.

"I see."

Robert looks to his father and back again at the general.

"I am sorry for my part in it," says the general. "I have done everything I could."

"I know you have."

"Waging war over the subject seems not to have been enough."

"Just so."

Grant scoffs. "We fought an entire war to lay this to rest."

"With respect, sir, we *settled* the war."

Grant smiles and offers a compromise. "We ended it."

"The Confederates went home."

"They had been punished sufficiently."

"Perhaps not."

"Some things carry more weight than punishment. Compassion carries more weight. Respect carries more weight. The reuniting of a splintered nation carries a good deal more weight."

"I do not doubt it for a minute."

"My charge was to unite this country, not to destroy half of it."

"It was both your charge and your natural inclination, Mr. President. You are a man of faith and forgiveness."

"Not faith," Grant scoffs.

"Faith in goodness, I mean. In the goodness of mankind. In the possibility of man's improving, given opportunity and encouragement. I ask you: Who else could have led an army to such a victory and come away with the admiration of both sides?"

"You're too kind."

"I am not. It is so. And the key to it, I believe, is that the men love you for the same reason they love Jesus. *You forgave them.* You forgave them without condition. Why, if the war were still on, you'd be fighting and forgiving them still."

Grant takes this for the compliment it would seem to be, and he will think about it often, until by and by Robert's words begin to open up to him like a night-blooming flower. Perhaps his gentler impulses were a failing from the start. Perhaps his strategic instincts served him for a while but tripped him up in the end. Perhaps he is both a calculating, heartless, vengeful brute and the possessor of a heart of gold.

In so contradictory a man would lie either great humanity or great wickedness. So it is with a divided nation.

Robert said, *You'd be fighting and forgiving them still.* It takes a sharp eye to observe such a truth, and a subtle mind to put it so delicately. He has not expected these qualities from a colored man, although for the life of him he cannot say why. He shall strive to be more attuned to such things in the future.

Forty Days and Forty Nights

His pain ebbs and his consciousness dims as the drug creeps through his bloodstream. Were he a healthier individual—his heartbeat strong, his breathing free, his nervous system functioning as the Almighty intended—this dose might be his last, for it would arrive at speed and strike like a locomotive. At this extremity, however, his failed systems conspire to act as a kind of governor or limiting valve. This, at least, is the opinion of Dr. Douglas, who can divine no other explanation for the man's increasing imperviousness.

Stubborn, this one. Stubborn as ever. Stubborn enough to finish that book, maybe—with the help of chemicals that would have killed a lesser man by now.

Douglas has herded the family off to supper with reassurances that the general will recover once the medicine finds its mark. They have trooped off with the best of intentions, and for the sake of the children they have spread blankets beneath the shade of the trees and tried making a picnic of it. Their attempts to cultivate gaiety die on the vine. Every voice is hushed and every conversation is hesitant. The children sit with their backs against the trunks of trees, listless, scattered and still as tombstones. Faithful old Sam Willett, stationed a dozen yards downhill and gnawing morosely at a drumstick supplied by his musical partner, little Julia, minds the perimeter with the look of a mortician nursing a rotten tooth.

Inside the cottage, Douglas draws the curtains as if his patient needs or would notice further buffering from the intrusions of the world. As he does so, Grant's breathing hesitates for just an instant.

The Ohio River is a mirror.

Nothing moves upon it. Neither light nor air disturbs it. No cloud shadow passes over it and no current ruffles its surface. No leaping fish or diving bird pierces the membrane by which it defines itself. No raft or canoe, no dinghy or tender, no pleasure craft or towboat or barge, makes use of it. No shore-bound, reed-masked fugitive secretly drinks from its margins or micturates into its shallows, and no straw-hatted boy drops his line into its potent mysterious depths.

Time has ceased to run upon it.

As for his own particular location, it is past reckoning. He might be atop a high riverside cliff. He might be cradled, cloud-borne, in the hand of the Almighty. He might be at some even more perilous height, dangling from the talons of the Adversary himself, called upon by that great deceiver to testify or plummet.

But his vantage is no matter. What counts is that his lodestone gaze is fixed across the river in the direction of the North Star, the plow, the drinking gourd. Across the Ohio toward Indiana. There is a mystery there, and beneath his gaze it unfolds in multiple directions and all at once.

*   *   *

Jule.

On that long-ago day in Louisville.

Crossing toward Indiana.

He sees her as she steps onto the New Albany riverbank from the deck of a waterborne conveyance that shifts its form even as he watches—rowboat, riverboat, raft—and as her foot strikes the liberating earth, the world explodes into a million separate shards. Each shard is a life, and she steps into them all.

She finds her way to a low tavern on a muddy waterfront lane and takes up work in the kitchen, where she endures the attentions of men of low habits and lower aims. Toil and misery and bodily peril are her fate until she dies from typhoid or at the hands of some roving miscreant or from any of a hundred other inevitable ills.

She seeks shelter—from the hammering rain or from the scorching sun, it makes no difference—beneath the overhanging eave of a church whose pastor, a circuit-riding Methodist just in from French Lick, welcomes her and finds her a place in the service of an antique spinster who one day will leave her a considerable share of a family fortune that no one, not even the pastor, knows she possesses. That same spinster does not die but goes mad instead and comes to despise her for her color or for some other reason and ends their relationship with a bottle of arsenic once obtained by Jule herself for killing rats.

She travels, the future advancing before her as the plow precedes the farmer, until she vanishes into the ramifying byways of a nation beyond the limits of the general's imagination.

She despairs.

She hopes.

She finds a love that is pure and true and endures forever. She finds a love that goes unrequited. She finds a love that proves faithless and from which she shall never recover.

She marries. She does not.

She dreams now and then of Julia, of the children and the grand-children, and even of the general himself. She does not dream of them even once but shuts them from her mind altogether rather than waste energy on the dead past.

She never has children of her own—not in any of her thousand times a thousand lives. Anything can happen to her but that, for too much time has passed. She has grown too old. It is a privation from any angle or height or distance. It is the unrestorable.

CHAPTER 12

1881–1882

Seduction

The ex-president rents offices—Number 2 Wall Street, second floor—
as a place to carry out some work he's been hired to do for the Mexican
Southern Railroad. The suite of rooms is modest. His office looks out
over the busy street and is decorated all around with trophies brought
home from his travels. Were you to ask him the origin of this painted
bamboo fan or that marble carving of an alien god, the ex-president
would delight in regaling you with a tale of its provenance, the longer and more filigreed the better. When the stories grow particularly
long—for these days he has the opportunity to speak not only of Chattanooga and the Wilderness but of Siam and Peru and locales even
more exotic, having been feted by potentates everywhere—there is
a dining room to the rear where he and his listeners may retreat for
fortification.

Capping off the arrangement is a hydraulic elevator that provides
an alternative to the stairs. The general is known to operate the works

himself, happy as a schoolboy to demonstrate the thing for visitors, feeling more like a railroad engineer than a former president of the United States.

No sooner has Grant moved in than his son's business associates—the young and charming Ferdinand Ward and the old and prickly James Fish, a mismatched pair of scoundrels alike only in their secret unappeasable lust for money—take offices directly below his. The sign upon their door reads "Grant & Ward." *Ward* means Ferdinand Ward, of course. *Grant* means callow young Buck Grant, Ulysses Jr., the general's middle son. If innocents in the world of finance should assume that the sign refers to the general himself, and conclude upon its evidence that he is of high rank in the firm, it is of no concern to Ward and Fish. Let the buyer beware. They operate an investment banking firm, not a Sunday school.

And thus do they hang like a pair of spiders in the darkness below Grant's rooms. They are implacable, secretive, patient. They have plans and they are in no hurry to reveal them. Creatures such as this are always to be found where men gather, weaving pale and sticky threads through the warp and weft of the daylit world. They are often much nearer to us than we know. One may be right alongside your boot just now. Look sharp or you'll miss it. No matter. It won't have gone far.

Grant pays these two gentlemen no mind as long as Buck is happy. And Buck is as happy as he can be, for Ward—known these days as the Young Napoleon of Wall Street—has a golden touch in a gilded age. Everything that he smiles upon blooms. If you were to put a ten-dollar bill into his left hand, you could take a twenty from his right and he would be none the poorer for it. He would hint, in fact, that he has made a profit on the transaction, although no one but Fish—and perhaps not even Fish—will see evidence of it.

It warms the old general's heart to see his son thriving. Buck and his wife, Fannie—daughter of a retired Colorado senator who has made his fortune in mining—are living now in a grand Manhattan town house given to them by the senator on their wedding day and decorated throughout with the excess of Grant's trophy collection. So plentiful is the overflow that certain less prized artifacts have found their way out the servants' entrance and straight into Ward's apartments on the other side of the city, whether Grant is aware of it or not. That armchair made from the horns of some four-legged denizen of the African plains? There can be no harm in letting visitors believe it was a gift from the ex-president, bestowed in appreciation for some act left tantalizingly undescribed.

Grant has never had a mind for finance. The fault lies in the poverty of his youth, for in childhood he was as likely to possess a fistful of pennies as he was to encounter the philosopher's stone. Money was a rare thing of arcane power, known mainly by its absence. The difficulty and peril of earning the slightest bit of it—usually amid the sickening fumes of his father's tannery—worked to cloud its usual relationship with labor. You could work all the livelong day and finish up with little or nothing.

His grasp of matters financial did not improve at West Point or in the army or in the White House, where he was insulated from them. Along the way, however, because the commonest link to power in America is the possession of money, he did acquire many wealthy friends and associates. When his presidency was done and it was either return to a humble Missouri farm or be lifted to the realm where society desired to ensconce him, certain of those friends laid plans to help. His glory reflected well upon theirs, after all, and it could not be trusted to do so from a place as far removed as Hardscrabble. So it was that gentlemen with names like Morgan and Vanderbilt—men whose fortunes owed nothing to the president—established a standing fund that should maintain him until death. The costs to them were insignificant, and it would not do to have the great man embarrassed.

He was only four years out of the White House when Buck fell in with Ferdinand Ward. Since those early days Grant has made damnably little progress on the Mexican Southern Railroad, but there have lately been some changes in his connection with his son's firm. The Young Napoleon of Wall Street has won battle after battle in his march toward the creation of incalculable wealth, delivering to himself and to his partners and to his investors a rate of return far outstripping the dreams of the most rabid speculator—and doing so with such clockwork regularity that one could almost describe an investment with him as *guaranteed*. No one in the banking business would dare use that forbidden term, of course. At least not in tones above a whisper.

The man is everywhere, his influence and intelligence reaching into every corner of the city's financial life. When Grant and Julia begin seeking out a brownstone on the East Side, he happens to know the ideal specimen, on Sixty-Sixth Street between Fifth and Madison. Ward himself sets aside his duties to the firm long enough to handle the transaction personally, out of kindness. With his help, Grant acquires the place—brand-new, too large and too elegant by half—for a figure considerably beneath the asking price. The money is withdrawn from the standing fund established by Morgan and Vanderbilt, which reduces its total by about a third.

To affirm his faith in his son's business, Grant is persuaded to come on as a partner. It requires a six-figure investment, exactly as much as Buck put in at the start, which depletes the remaining rainy-day fund by about half. No matter. The reduction is far surpassed by its value in goodwill. *Thank God, he thinks, that Buck and Ward have been in partnership for a considerable period. Otherwise, people might assume that I am the Grant whose name is on the letterhead.*

Buck's father-in-law, the retired Senator Chaffee, makes the same investment in return for a partnership of his own, although from his perspective the amount at stake is trivial. There is always more in the mines.

With the general on board comes paperwork galore. Some days he signs thirty or forty letters, although he never spares the time to read them. He is too busy with visitors and cigars and catered luncheons in his private dining room. Ward hires a young clerk who wears out a pair of shoes every eight weeks on the stairs to Grant's office, carrying correspondence to be signed with the general's hand. Grant does not permit him to use the elevator, believing that it will set a habit sure to make him soft.

Grant's first visitor every morning is young Ward himself, bearing a bundle of twenty-five cigars bound up like so many roses. It is all the general can do to use them up by day's end, and he manages only by staying close to his desk and applying himself without letup. The sight and the smell of them bring him back to Fort Donelson and the rage that followed for sending him cigars by the half ton, and he retails that familiar story to Ward on more than a few occasions. The cigars trigger both his memory of the war and his affection for the men who were once under his command, sending him hurtling back through the bewildering mists of time to a place of great clarity. He never once thinks that Ward might intend these tokens as something in the way of an investment.

Forty Days and Forty Nights

Dent placed the loss at his son-in-law's feet, of course. The disappearance of that confounded slave girl and everything that either led up to it or followed from it, back to the creation and forward to the end of time. All of it was Grant's fault.

He can hear the colonel raging even now, seething away in his memory:

How is White Haven to manage with another slave gone?

White Haven won't miss her. She worked at Hardscrabble. She worked for Julia.

She belonged to me. I shall require restitution.

I shall pay it.

Full value, and no mistake.

Absolutely.

Value which I shall set according to the usual principles.

After the Emancipation, her value will be mainly to herself.

The Emancipation has not yet come to this state.

It will arrive soon enough.

Thanks to you.

Thanks to President Lincoln.

The girl would not have escaped had you and Julia been traveling together.

I was seeing to the nation's business.

Curse the nation's business. It serves only to pick my pocket.

The man's grievances know no limit, and in the chambers of Grant's brain they echo round without ceasing. They tangle and they twist and they multiply, each one leading into another, however tangentially related. Grant must summon all of his resources of concentration to sever their thread, dam their flow. He must drive them from his mind if he is to return to his work.

As always, the electricity shuts down at ten o'clock. Terrell could set his watch by it if he owned a watch. In the dark he rises from the porch step; he has been listening to the faint strains of a string quartet imported from New York for some formal affair at the Balmoral, watching the hotel's lights glimmer through the trees like the last semaphore of a dying civilization. With a sigh he steps inside to light the lamps. The brief interval between the electrical present and the flame-lit past carries for him a great weight.

The general and Mrs. Grant have been conversing in the parlor, he beneath a blanket in his upholstered sleeping chair, she in an old rocker pulled up close and squeaking like a mouse living beneath the floorboards. Now that the electric light has died, their talk will be impeded a bit, and it has been a halting affair to begin with — the general writing out his thoughts on slips of paper, his wife whispering low in return as if to match the soft, slow rhythm set by the pencil. They commune in this way as if they have all the time in the world.

Terrell strikes a lucifer and acknowledges the two of them in its flare. He lights lamps in opposite corners of the room and then proceeds to attend to the remainder of the cottage, trailing light as he goes.

Grant is in a mood best described as reflective, and the enveloping dark does nothing to diminish it. It seems to him the ancient dark of his boyhood, the relentless dark of Hardscrabble, the foreboding dark of a canvas tent erected at the edge of some contested battlefield. He is at home in every instance of it, and he wishes none of it away.

As he bends over the lap desk, the letters emerge upon his little slip of paper like things conjuring themselves from the shadows. There is magic and mystery in their appearance, and when they are all present he slides the paper toward her across a little valley in the blanket.

It reads, *Do you still think of Jule?*

She purses her lips in the gloom, considering. "I doubt that she thinks of me."

A tolerant smile slips invisibly to his face and then steals just as invisibly away. *I shouldn't think reciprocity would be required.*

"I suppose not. Nonetheless."

You don't wonder what became of her?

"I prefer to think of her as she was. She was a favorite, after all. Very nearly a member of the family."

Very nearly. He almost adds the question mark but does not.

"As nearly as could be. She had been loyal from the beginning."

She was loyal until she could endure being loyal no longer.

She stiffens. "Until loyalty no longer suited her."

Her husband frowns beneath his mustache. *What she did required great bravery, I think.*

"She should have gone with me to White Haven. It would have

been the considerate thing, given Fred's typhoid. I went mad with worry about both of them."

He lets it pass.

"President Lincoln had already secured her future. It would have been only a matter of weeks."

She feared your father.

"Didn't we all?"

She had the courage to escape him first.

CHAPTER 13

1883

Accounting

Ward's reputation grows. Rumor has it that he has achieved dazzling new heights via speculation on the Produce Exchange. It is a risky enterprise, one where men of iron nerve and lightning judgment often go down to ruin, but it is a bagatelle for Ward. He is always ready for each turn of the market, always prepared to capitalize on opportunities that other investors might not observe until the moment for action has passed. His investments perform so brilliantly and with such consistency that they distract observers from whatever form their mechanics might actually take. Who knows, moment by moment, what he is investing in or how? His secret, some say, is that he has acquired special insights into government contracts regarding the goods in question. And if he should happen to glance meaningfully up toward the former president's offices as he hands a check to one of the chosen, who is to be the wiser? Certainly not Ulysses S. Grant, for Ward tells him no more than Captain Kidd told his figurehead.

Investors would shun the enterprise if there weren't so much money to be made. The chief condition of their doing business with Ward is that any possibility of the general's influence must go unsaid, for whether he is innocent or complicit, to let it be known that you suspect his involvement in such a scheme would be to dishonor him. In this way, as the months go by and the returns add up, a cloud of charitable silence comes to envelop the general. It is invisible to him by design.

Buck's father-in-law comes east in search of ways to invest the riches that continue to pour from the mouths of his Colorado mines. He and his wife lodge in one of their magnificent New York houses, in rooms suited to emperors or demigods, and for a period of two or three weeks they circulate vigorously among Chaffee's old associates in government and business. They are feted in grand houses and they dine out in fine restaurants and they attend a wide variety of stiflingly dull theatrical performances. All the while, Chaffee keeps his ear to the ground.

He is listening for opportunity, and he hears the same information again and again. *Grant & Ward.* The firm's name is on everyone's lips. He wonders at first if the talk is mere flattery regarding his daughter's choice of a husband, but over time the theme proves commonplace and consistent. Men he trusts and men upon whom he would not risk a penny put their faith in Grant & Ward with equal enthusiasm. Secretive men who trace their fortunes to shadowy connections in faraway countries have no less confidence in him than do the scribblers who write his lavish praise in the newspapers.

Grant & Ward. Grant & Ward. Grant & Ward.

To invest elsewhere is to throw your money away.

Still, Chaffee knows that he ought to have more insight into the operation. Business is business and family is family, so it seems a trifle indelicate to press his own son-in-law too closely. There is another avenue, of course: Ward himself. And he has a plausible reason for inquiring: the precise state of his original investment.

He catches Ward first thing one morning, hurrying down the stairs from the general's office.

"The two of us put our heads together each day at this time," says Ward, lifting his eyes up to the heavens, from whence his help cometh. "Such *intelligence* he possesses!"

"*Intelligence?*" Doubting not the word but Ward's particular use of it.

"Intelligence. I could hardly do business without the old rascal."

"*Rascal?* I shouldn't think—"

"Perhaps you don't know him as well as I."

Chaffee scoffs. He and Grant know each another quite well, thank you, but Ward only gives back a fawning smile. "At any rate," says Chaffee, "I'm almost embarrassed to make so trivial a request, but do you suppose I could obtain a current statement?"

A questioning look from Ward.

"A statement—regarding my shares in the firm. The usual thing. Their value over time and so forth. The details of their whereabouts. I mean a proper full accounting, rather than your usual summary."

"Are you thinking of selling, Senator?"

"Why, not at all. And as I remember, there were conditions on any such—"

"Conditions, yes. We wouldn't want to dilute the pool of ownership, would we?"

"No, of course not."

"We'd like to keep things in the family."

"Yes."

"That said, I'm certain that if you *were* to sell, the other shareholders and I would be happy to reacquire your shares. Perhaps you're a bit short of funds at the moment?"

"Hardly."

"Have you lost confidence in the firm?"

"Oh, no," says Chaffee. "Never."

A thin and faintly mistrustful smile from Ward. "Very well. I shall ask Mr. Cooper to prepare a statement. Might you return for it at week's end?"

He might and he does. Mr. Cooper is the head of accounting at Grant & Ward, and his name and seal are on the document, although his hand has been nowhere in its vicinity. The work is all Ward's. The information arrayed on these pages in columns and rows is a riot of numbers, names, and dates. Transactions are recorded in code—digits and characters all jumbled up, with here and there a Greek letter or a symbol that looks like a sort of Egyptian hieroglyph tossed in for good measure—a code that can be translated only with the help of a little leather-bound book that Ward keeps in a secret drawer.

"We cannot be too careful about this information," he says, brandishing the little volume. "We cannot keep it too close. These are government contracts, for the most part, and our unquestioned access to them is critical to our success."

Without the little book, the identifiers are nonsense. With the little book, they reveal a system of investments that infiltrates the deepest workings of city, state, and federal government. As Ward flips briskly through the pages, Chaffee glimpses columns headed "livestock" and "public lands," "telegraphy" and "int'l. trade," "Indian settlements" and "Nicaragua."

Suggestive as these details might be, his attention drifts away from them. It settles instead on the statement lying fanned out in the sunlight upon Ward's desk—in particular on the rightmost column of each page, where a running total just keeps going up and up and up.

Ward notices. "Getting right down to brass tacks," he says, putting a finger on the column in question and palming the little book at the same time. Chaffee will never see its shadow again. "Essentials, Senator. That's the ticket! Our investors are men with little time for details. They entrust the finely grained work to us, just as long as the returns keep piling up."

Piling up is an entirely accurate phrase, in Chaffee's mind, and he says so.

"Wall Street has high expectations for Grant & Ward, and we have not disappointed yet."

Chaffee separates the pages and studies them one after another. "There has not been a single misstep, according to these records. Not in, what, nearly four years?"

"Just so."

"It is a miracle."

"It is the product of hard work. Hard work and unmatched *intelligence*."

"But, Ward, the value of my shares has grown sevenfold."

"Sevenfold and a trifle more." Ward points to the total. "I have consulted with the other partners," he says, "and we would be willing to buy back your shares as presently valued. In case you have lost faith in our methods, I mean. Fair is fair. We wouldn't dream of keeping you—or your money—prisoner."

Chaffee draws a handkerchief from his pocket and mops his brow. "What would I do with it then? What other investment could perform half so well?"

Ward lifts an eyebrow.

Chaffee inhales. "Very well," he says. "I should like to quadruple my investment."

"Quadruple your *original* investment, or quadruple its *current* value?"

Chaffee does not falter. "Quadruple the current value," he says, pocketing the handkerchief and reaching for his checkbook. "Most assuredly."

The look that passes across Ward's face must resemble the one worn by the God of Abraham upon the completion of the world. He masks it quickly and completely, however, and Chaffee is too busy writing out his check to take notice.

Grant does his best to seem unsurprised when Chaffee offers to light his cigar with a bill of large denomination, and he covers well enough by inveighing for a few moments against the destruction of negotiables entrusted to private citizens by the United States of America, but his heart is not in it. Riches such as those Chaffee has reported—riches beyond the dreams of avarice—are beyond his imagining as well. Had you asked Grant how much his investment had earned to date, he would have guessed five or ten percent. Surely not seven hundred or more.

He leaps to invest the remainder of his standing fund, and then he begins a campaign to convert everyone he knows to the profitable church of Grant & Ward. It is a siege worthy of General Bragg. He hounds his sons Fred and Jesse until they turn over every cent to their brother. He plagues his British son-in-law, the insufferable Sartoris, until he converts the bulk of his accumulated pounds sterling into dollars—not Irish whiskey, which would seem to be his usual—and wires them off to Buck for multiplication. No family member is beyond his reach. Far-flung aunts and uncles, cousins from first to third and variously removed, nieces and nephews without number and regardless of means, find themselves invited to share in the wealth.

At home, he expands Julia's generous personal and household allowances until she barely has time to spend them. She does her best, however, and he has never felt better on that count. He accompanies her on shopping trips as often as his schedule permits. The finest that Manhattan has to offer in the way of furniture, home goods, apparel for ladies and gentlemen, and luxury merchandise from all around the globe waits just outside their door. There was a time when the general was reluctant to present himself at such places, for merchants were always and forever reducing their prices out of respect for the savior of the Union. It came to be downright embarrassing. But now, once the day's expedition is plotted, he sends a boy ahead with a message: *President Grant appreciates your kindness, and he insists on paying full price.*

The house blooms under Julia's redoubled care. To make room for all of the new furniture, the old is either shuttled off to the attics or given away. Buck has no use for any of it, since between his own wealth and the largesse of his father-in-law his own town house is as crowded with merchandise as the hold of a tramp steamer. Ward continues to take the overflow, often as not. He has certain interests that ensure he will always find a good home for these, the very grandest of castoffs.

Late one winter afternoon, after the last of the deliverymen have gone, Grant catches his wife studying her reflection in the mirror newly set up in her dressing room. It is most unusual, this focus on herself, and he lingers unseen in the hallway to observe it. She would ordinarily prefer to look at anything but her own reflection. Even in photographs she has always looked askance, turning her face from the camera at a slight angle so as to make herself a touch invisible, the least bit beyond fully capturing. The fault is in her eyes, which have been crossed since girlhood.

Knowing his wife as well as he does, he guesses that she was admiring the new mirror, a splendid object in an ornate carved frame brought from the Black Forest, when her attention drifted from the thing itself to the reflection within it. The light from the west-facing windows illuminates her face with a direct tenderness that strikes him to the heart. Whatever it has cost him to arrive at this moment—this house, this window, this mirror, this low gleam of sun—has been worth doing. He sighs, and she takes note, and his momentary secrecy is gone.

"As lovely as ever," he observes.

"Which is saying precious little."

"Don't deprive me of that joy." He enters the room and settles upon the bench alongside his wife. "Please." He says the word with his blue eyes fixed on hers, and upon his lips that earnest smile that still weakens her, forty years on and then some.

"I shall be seeing a new surgeon next month," she says, returning her gaze to the mirror and her intractable eye. "An eye specialist from Boston, here to lecture on the latest."

"Have there been advances?"

"Some. But perhaps not for an old woman like me. We shall see what he recommends."

"You do recall my position on the subject?"

"I do. Quite clearly."

"I should hate to see you altered in any way."

"*Oh, Ulysses,*" she says. As if he could not possibly mean such a thing. "You are such a great figure, and I am so plain."

"Perhaps I shouldn't care for the new Mrs. Grant."

She gives him a mischievous look. "Now you're being ridiculous."

Of course he is. He smiles at her again, and her gaze drifts perilously back toward her reflection in the mirror, and he takes her hand. They remain exactly that way, a fresh tableau of something eternal, until the color fades from the window and Terrell knocks upon the door, seeking to light the lamps.

The doctor from Boston comes in November, and his counsel is that Julia would have best profited from his new findings perhaps fifty years previous. "Leave perfection to the young," he says. "It is a fantasy beyond the grasp of mortals like you and me."

She is still smarting with disappointment when Thanksgiving arrives to distract her. The day is clear, blue, and fine, and the general presides over a sumptuous noontime table with a dozen loved ones gathered all around. Their faces are so bright that he cannot resist crediting himself a little for the occasion.

"Let us thank our Maker for this nourishment," he says, putting on a pious face. "And while we're doing so, let us thank the gentleman at the head of the table for signing the Holidays Act, without which this good food would be going to waste."

"Oh, Ulys," says Julia. "You'd think you were John Alden himself."

Her husband gives back a hurt look that cannot last.

The merriment lasts until Christmas Eve. Winter has settled in during the prior week, starting with high winds and frigid temperatures and ending with a steady snowfall that blankets the city into stillness, quieting its commotion and softening its edges. It is late in the afternoon on the twenty-fourth, and high-spirited carolers and shoppers contend for mastery of the streets. Central Park, gaslit, is a wonderland. At home on Sixty-Sixth Street, Julia is preparing to receive visitors—three children and their spouses, along with a full complement of rambunctious grandchildren—while Grant himself is setting out to do some visiting of his own. His coachman has brought the carriage around, and Grant, the soul of generosity, reaches into his pocket to retrieve a little bundle of bills he has tucked away for the man's holiday gift. "A merry Christmas to you, Grayson!" he shouts, placing one foot on the icy iron step and reaching up to hand the bundle to the driver and in the process losing his balance. Down he goes to the icy ground, hard on his shoulder and hip, sliding to a stop halfway beneath the carriage.

Grayson leaps to his rescue, the folded bills vanishing into a snowbank to be retrieved God knows when by God knows whom. With the reins fallen slack, the horses go still as cast bronze. Once on the ground, Grayson has difficulty with the icy footing himself. It is all he can do to edge the general out from between the wheels.

"Forgive me," says Grant once he is in the clear, painfully ashamed to be the source of any inconvenience. He groans and rights himself onto his better hip and reaches up for Grayson's hand, but his shoulder pains him and will not take his weight. "Get Harrison," he says, wincing and lowering himself back onto the frozen ground.

Harrison. The driver has never heard Grant refer to the man by his first name alone. *Harrison.* Not *Terrell* and not the vaguely demeaning *Faithful Harrison*, just *Harrison*, plain and simple. As if they were equals or old comrades.

The driver goes to the front door and summons Terrell, who flies to the general's rescue minus his coat, hat, and gloves. Minus his customary dignity. Minus everything but compassion. He bends to Grant's aid but finds that he lacks the strength to lift him. The two in these late years have become a matched and increasingly useless pair, falling to pieces side by side.

The driver hurries over and together they fetch the general indoors, and Julia sends for the doctor while they wrestle him up the stairs. He will be confined to his bedroom until springtime. Theories will abound as to the nature of his injury. It is a severed tendon. It is a broken bone. It is a torn muscle. Never mind which diagnosis or combination of diagnoses might be accurate; not one of them will help him recover. The fact is that he has reinjured the very hip that tormented him in New Orleans twenty years ago. Two decades and two presidential terms and the never-ending Great War of the Rebellion have intervened since then.

He misses the pageant of life on Wall Street. The torrent of correspondence to be signed, the steady stream of admirers, the catered luncheons, the visits from Ward with his daily bundle of cigars. At this stage in life, serving as a partner at Grant & Ward suits him better than serving as the president of the United States—or even as commanding general of the U.S. Army. He is just another foot soldier now, content to do his modest part and leave the great strategic matters to his superiors. He has earned that much. Thank heavens he can count upon Buck and Ward to keep the wheels of commerce turning. That thought cheers him, but not enough to entirely offset the doldrums that come with being marooned in his bedchamber.

Julia has an idea. He ought to try his hand at writing out his memoirs. She can equip him with paper and pens and a portable desk for use in his bed. She would even take dictation, should he prefer to get the facts down that way. But he is a difficult customer.

"The facts are well-known already. They have been in the newspapers and they will one day be in the history books."

"Why did your friend Sherman bother, then?" She means William Tecumseh Sherman, whose recent memoirs everyone seems to have read.

Grant has paged through some of Sherman's book and found it commendable but wanting. He gives Julia a wink and observes, "Uncle Billy has his own way of seeing things."

"And you don't?"

"He would like to be remembered in a certain way, I suspect."

"And you wouldn't?"

"I'd like to be remembered for what I have done, not for how I might dress it up in prose." He winces at a sudden stab of pain from his hip, looks out the window, and wearies instantly of the familiar view. "Besides, I am no Clemens with a pen."

"I should hope not. The truth isn't in that man." She says it with the affection that Clemens's tall tales have cultivated in readers all over the world.

Grant barks a laugh and she leaves off, satisfied to have perhaps planted the seed of an idea in her husband's brain. As the days go by, she will encourage and cultivate that seed in many small ways. She leaves Sherman's book among the reading materials at his bedside. She provides supplies of writing materials so vast that her husband could not use them up with correspondence in a lifetime. After a while she exchanges Sherman's book for her husband's dog-eared copy of Julius Caesar's *Commentaries on the Civil War*. She buys him a handsome fountain pen of lapis lazuli and says that in the hubbub surrounding his fall she neglected to give it to him at Christmas.

"You are not half so subtle as you think," he says as she slips out of her bed one dark winter morning.

"I'm sorry I've awoken you."

"It isn't that. It's that blasted writing project. You won't let it go."

"I haven't mentioned it in a month, Ulys. You said you weren't interested."

"And yet you continue to think of nothing else."

She strikes a lucifer and holds it to the little brass lamp on the mantelpiece. By its glow he sees her plain.

"Is it not so? Tell me, Julia."

Her look is a confession.

"Very well," he says. "If it so important to you, I shall consider it. I shall consider it directly."

She would tell him all the million reasons her heart and mind and soul want it done, but they are unnecessary now. Besides, confronted too bluntly at this moment, he might reconsider.

He begins at the beginning, in the manner of the Creator Himself.

The year is 1630. The place is Dorchester, Massachusetts. The stranger arriving on the scene—for every story worth telling begins with the arrival of a stranger at some dockside or train station or wilderness outpost—is Matthew Grant, founder of the family in America. Thus does the general commit from the start to making his *Memoirs* an American book, with his family as its foundation and his nation as its frame.

He does not intend to make himself the center of it—he would remain out of focus and off to one side if he could—but soon he has run short of history and we have arrived at West Point and the die is cast.

"I plan to address my education only to set the stage for what comes afterward," he tells Julia. "My aim will be to vanish entirely from my accounts of both the Mexican War and the Great War of the Rebellion. Educating the reader first as to what I learned at West Point—matters of strategy, for example, and the history of war—will provide the context necessary to understand the action, eliminating the need for bringing personality into it."

"These are *memoirs*, Ulys. They're supposed to be personal."

"Bosh."

"Your battlefield reports are in the public record, if anyone wants to read them."

"These will all be in one place."

"I think you're missing an opportunity."

"We shall see."

"People will want a look into your mind."

"They can tell its workings by the evidence of history. A man doesn't need to take his watch apart in order to learn the time."

"You're expecting too much."

"I think not."

"You're giving too little."

"Not by any means." He pats the papers at his side. "I have already given everything, Julia. These scraps are what is left behind."

"We shall see," she says, believing that he may need to try his hand at this enterprise before he realizes how much he has to learn.

Forty Days and Forty Nights

How is he to write in the presence of so many infernal admirers? He cannot just put his back to them and go about his business. With Willett on guard duty down the hill, those who get through are generally associates or friends of long standing. Men of elevated position, deserving of his respect even as he battles through this last campaign.

He owes them something, yet he is not a mere performing beast, a dancing bear or a trained lion ready to pirouette or stand upon his hind legs for a portion of raw meat. The fact is that he can barely stand on his own legs at all. Not for more than a moment or two, after which he is certain to be so spent that he will be unable to write for a period of time too precious to spare.

It pains him to consider his immobility, but he cannot deny it. Whether he is seated in his wheeled chair on the porch like a houseplant set out for air or sunken into his upholstered chair in the parlor like a mummy settled into its sarcophagus, he is a desolated curiosity. Add to that his precipitous loss of weight, the spastic quivering of his hands, the blankets under which he comforts his shivering body, and the heavy scarves with which he conceals his swollen neck, and the result is a figure to be pitied. Not a man but a vessel—a vessel cracked and broken, a ruined Roman aqueduct through which the memories preserved in his mind creep onto the page.

He desires only the company of family. Julia to hover over him like the veriest angel. Fred to do the business of checking his memories against the record. Buck and Jesse and their wives to wrangle the grandchildren. Nellie to lift him up as only a daughter can. This is all he needs in the world—all he needs beyond Dr. Douglas and Harrison Terrell, that is, Faithful Harrison, a nurse by assignment and a companion by history and inclination—and he is fortunate to have them all gathered here in this cottage at the end of time.

Fortunate. How foolish to use the word even in the private sanctity of his own mind. He would laugh if laughter were possible, but his voice has been failing him of late. He parcels out the use of it just as he has learned to parcel out every other precious thing. Soon he shall be stoppered up for good, reduced to writing out his thoughts and needs on slips of paper.

Mostly now he speaks to his wife and children of the great and undying love he has for each of them. What else is there? He would rather not mention the additional matter that occupies his mind: the family's two possible destinies. Comfort if he succeeds in his work, woe if he fails.

Victory on one hand, defeat on the other.

Such is the war he fights now, and in settling it he must admit no compromise.

CHAPTER 14

1884

Revelation

Eventually he escapes from his confinement and takes to the streets with the help of a cane. Manhattan welcomes him with five hundred tipped hats for every thousand smiles, and spring welcomes him with an early arrival. The streets and the skies open up on the same schedule, as if both the city and Mother Nature wish the celebrated general no further harm.

The clear sailing lasts about a month.

On a Sunday morning in early May he takes a visit from Buck's partner. To judge from Ward's disheveled state, he would seem to have been up all night. He has a broken, plaintive look written upon him, and the hopeful gleam that still burns in his eye only serves to accentuate it. The contrast gives him the ghastly air of a ravenous corpse.

"I hate to bother you on the Lord's day," he begins.

"The Lord created all seven days," says Grant, "and they are equal to me. I do not discriminate." He has never felt much passion for religion. Julia, for her part, is at church right now, listening to a sermon from their old Washington associate, Rev. John Philip Newman, and most of the household staff has scattered to their various houses of worship as well. Until the moment when Ward crossed the threshold, Grant and Terrell have had the brownstone to themselves.

"I am afraid that we are in a bit of a pinch," says Ward.

"A pinch?"

"A pinch. A bit of one."

"A bit of a pinch."

"Yes. A bit of a financial pinch, I'm afraid to say."

Ward seems reluctant to speak the words out loud, as if saying them might bring down some fate even worse. Such hesitance from a man with so persuasive a tongue! Grant finds the prospect unsettling. "Out with it," he says.

"I'm embarrassed to trouble you with it on this fine morning . . ."

"Out with it, I say."

"And I wouldn't bother you in person, of course, but Buck is in church and Mr. Fish is nowhere to be found—"

"Fish is an enigma."

"He is our connection with the banks."

"He is nonetheless an enigma. Regardless, I should think he and Buck would be in their offices tomorrow. We must put our heads together then."

"Tomorrow," says a wistful Ward. "Yes. If only the matter would wait that long."

Grant aims a look at him. "Now, I'm just an old soldier and an out-of-work politician," he says, "but for the life of me I can't imagine what kind of financial business might get done on a Sunday."

"The essential kind," says Ward, taking a handkerchief from his pocket and wringing it as if it might contain something of value.

"Essential?"

"The kind that goes on between men, not between institutions."

If ever a statement were custom-tailored to arouse Grant's natural instincts, Ward has hit upon it, for at each turning of the man's life—as son, brother, student, soldier, husband, father, grandfather, general, and president—he has accepted all burdens as personal acts of service. A little bubble of emotion rises up in his chest now at the thought: *I can surely resolve this, if anyone can.* So certain is he of his competence that for an instant he nearly misses the size of the task before him.

"We need nearly a half million," says Ward. "By tomorrow morning."

The little bubble pops and leaves him breathless.

"I have personally located sources for most of it, thank God. But we are still one hundred and fifty thousand short."

Grant is dumbfounded, and looks it.

"It is a banking matter. Just a little inconvenience of bookkeeping, really."

"A *little inconvenience.*"

"It is as if two letters have crossed in the mail. That sort of thing. A narrowly missed connection. It can be resolved in a moment."

"I see."

"Fish's other firm, the Marine Bank, is where the mishap occurred. One of their larger investors—the City of New York—suddenly requires the half million I mentioned. Payable tomorrow, free and clear. Alas, the Marine Bank is still waiting for another transaction to close. And thus they are temporarily embarrassed."

"How temporarily?"

"A day. Perhaps two." He counts on his fingers. "Yes, two. Two at the most."

"And how thoroughly embarrassed?"

"If caused to produce the amount in question, the Marine Bank would go belly up."

"*Belly up*. Leave it to a fish."

Ward smiles. "Just so, General. Just so. Alas, since they are entrusted with all of our holdings, we would fail along with them."

"Everything might go to ruin—for want of a day's grace?"

"I could not have put it better myself."

"A matter of hours, really?"

"Hours," says Ward, nodding like an old sage. "Minutes, you could say."

"I have won and lost terrible battles in such small amounts of time, but I have always entered the field at the ready. This, however! It has arisen so suddenly!"

"That is the nature of business."

"I haven't the stomach for it. Not any longer."

Ward nods as if he is positively made of sympathy. He knows that however strenuously Grant might object, he will not fail in the end.

The general cogitates. "Can the city be put off?"

"They would lose faith in Grant & Ward. And as their sentiments go, so go the sentiments of all of our investors. We should be ruined either way."

"Might we get a loan from another institution?"

"Not in time. And not with what looks like an empty cashbox for collateral."

"Even for so short a period?"

"Would *you* loan money to an operation like ours? An operation on the verge of failure?"

"Grant & Ward is *not* on the verge of failure."

"To an outsider, it would seem to be."

"Rubbish," says Grant.

"You and I know differently, and that is why we must look to ourselves."

Grant chews at his mustache. "Thank heaven you have already raised most of it. If you've come for a personal investment on my part, though, I must tell you the obvious: everything I have is already in the firm."

"Sadly, that is the case for all of us. You and I, Buck and Fish. We have given it our all."

"There is a fifth partner, don't forget. Chaffee. Chaffee has boundless resources."

"Is he in the city these days?"

"I believe he is at home in Colorado."

Ward gives his foot a little stamp of frustration. "His fortune, then, is out of our reach. We cannot tolerate the delays imposed by distance."

"No matter," says Grant. "I know another. The richest man in America lives quite close by."

"Vanderbilt?"

"Yes. he is an old friend and a generous one."

"Will you go to him for us?" says Ward. "My dignity would never survive the public confession of so small an error with such dire consequences."

"I will."

"Straight off? Right now?"

"Soon. The very instant Grayson returns and prepares the carriage."

Ward frowns. "But Vanderbilt's house, as you said, is quite close by."

"You seem to have forgotten my leg troubles."

"I daresay there can be little harm in walking a block or two."

"And I daresay there will be less harm in going by carriage."

Ward exchanges a sympathetic smile with the old man, but after an instant he lets it crumble.

"What if Vanderbilt steps out in the meantime?" he says, his face going white. "Whatever shall we do then?"

Grant rises and takes up his cane.

"I care nothing about the Marine Bank," says William Vanderbilt, once Grant has said what little needs to be said. "To tell the truth, I care very little about Grant & Ward. But to accommodate you personally, I will draw my check for the amount you need. It shall be a loan to you and to no one else."

Thus it is done, and such is the limit of it. There is no paper record, no contract, no collateral, no receipt. Just a check in the amount of one hundred fifty thousand dollars, payable to Ulysses S. Grant.

Not since Lincoln entrusted him with the nation's army has he felt a burden so heavy, so intimate, so unrelenting. It weighs him down and slows his steps on the walk home. When he arrives, he finds Ward anxiously pacing outside the front door. As if they have prearranged a signal, Grant pats his breast pocket and the Young Napoleon leaps for joy.

Monday proves uneventful. Grant arrives at his office on his usual schedule, signs his usual paperwork, and smokes his usual cigars. He dines with a retired Ohio congressman and a distinguished old colonel from Florida. The colonel made his fortune in the turpentine camps, upon the backs of black prisoners lucky enough to have been emancipated for just that purpose.

Ward is in his office, as is the enigmatic Fish. The transfer of Vanderbilt's funds between them must have gone well enough, for neither gives any sign of the slightest bother. Grant admires the two of them for that. To have come so near catastrophe and behave as if it were nothing is the mark of a cool head, and a cool head is a thing to be prized. Grant himself has always been said to possess a great, grave calm in the face of trouble, but that was on the battlefield of men. The battlefield of money is different. He lights a pensive cigar and looks out the window and reflects on the matter. Perhaps it is his ignorance of things financial that makes him so anxious in that area. He learned the art of war at West Point, a very long time ago, and despite the passing of the years that business has not changed much. War is all about men and might and movement. Find your enemy and know his strengths and assail him with everything you have. By comparison, finance seems to him a good deal closer to gambling. He would rather risk a thousand men against a known artillery emplacement than a thousand dollars against a roll of the dice.

Yet he has prevailed in this new world. He ought to be pleased.

If he felt any privation most acutely during the war—besides his separation from Julia, that is—it was the cursed shortage of coffee. It pained him as it pained his men, and he suffered right alongside them. These days he has the stuff in whatever quantities he might require. The cup standing upon his desk just now contains a dose black and syrupy enough to fortify the roughest frontiersman, and he sips it to start the day's usual round: coffee, newspaper, and cigars in equal parts. The cigars, alas, are not forthcoming, even after the newspaper has been read entire and the coffeepot is empty. There is in fact no sign of Ward today whatsoever, and so he calls for the young clerk and inquires as to his whereabouts.

"We ain't seen hide nor hair of him, sir." He is winded from racing up the stairs.

"'Hide nor hair'?" says Grant with a broad smile. "Let me tell you about 'hide nor hair.' I came of age in my father's tannery, you know." The reminiscences come freely these days. Anything can trigger them.

The boy grins back. "Begging your pardon, sir, I thought you came of age on Mount Olympus. To judge from your reputation, I mean."

"Nonsense," says Grant. By God, the boy is turning into a regular sycophant. No doubt he has been studying under Ward for too long. He shoos him away with instructions to bring word when the fellow arrives, and he never, ever sees him again. To be fair, he and the young clerk are not the only people who will spend the day looking for Ward, and by midmorning the offices are in such chaos that it's impossible to say exactly who's coming and who's going.

The long and short of it is that the Marine Bank has defaulted on the payment due the city, and a rough accounting has found its assets insufficient to provide so much as a one-way ticket to Staten Island aboard Cornelius Vanderbilt's ferry. Its funding gone, Grant & Ward has in turn collapsed. William Vanderbilt's lifesaving check for $150,000 has disappeared without a trace. The fortune that Ward claimed to have raised two days ago has proven a sham.

Over the next few days, more banks will fail and more investment houses will close. A complete accounting will take months, but in the end there will be tens of millions of dollars lost. Grant's every investment, and the investments of his friends and his associates and his family, will have turned to dust.

Despite the loud throng of panicked traders and bankers and financiers cramming the premises, Ward and Fish's private rooms stand as lifeless as exhibits from the destruction of Pompeii. Whatever went on there goes on no more, and the artifacts left behind cannot begin to tell the real story. As for the villains themselves, they seem to have retreated somewhere beyond the reach of mortal man. They are a pair of ghosts, gone slinking off into the dark spaces between worlds. Inquiries at their houses go unanswered. Pulls upon their doorbells go ignored. When night falls, no leak of lamp glow or candlelight escapes their quarters to betray the least trace of human presence.

When he steps down from the carriage to the sidewalk at home, he feels an instant's urge to drop down and ransack the bushes in search of the bills he lost back in December. The snow is gone, and the little leaves are beginning to show themselves, and if it weren't half-dark already, he might just fall to his knees and give it a try.

If only he could go back and do everything differently. Every dollar he has spent, he would unspend. Every penny he has thrown aside, he would collect and conserve for the days ahead.

It is just as well that he does not go to his knees now. With his bad hip and his advancing age and this new impossible emptiness in his chest that has been pulsing there since Ward and Fish's scheme came to light, he might never come upright again. The world is black and the days ahead are blacker. He can detect no way through them. He draws a deep breath and tips his hat to Grayson, outlined up on his box against the pale gray of the moon.

His salvation shall be Julia, as always.

She is waiting for him in the entryway, and he tells her the whole truth before she can guess it from his broken look. "I have lost everything we had," he says. "Absolutely everything."

Supper is waiting and he cannot eat it and yet he does. Nothing must go to waste now. Every grain of flour and every ounce of lamp oil and every shred of reputation must be husbanded.

"We have come up from nothing before," his wife tells him, "and we shall do it again. We can think of it as a return to Hardscrabble."

"*Hardscrabble*," he says, shaking his head as if to clear it of a dream.

Hardscrabble. "It would be like the old days," he says, picking up her thread, thinking the unthinkable with a little humorous gleam in his blue eyes. "I could take up my old trade in firewood. How about that? Do you suppose there's much call for it in New York anymore?"

"You'd need a woodlot," she says. "And an axe."

"An axe, yes. But a woodlot? I think I could do without one." He casts his gaze around the dining room, taking in the heavy walnut furniture and the framed portraits on the walls and the irreplaceable souvenirs of his travels on display in every corner. "There is lumber and rubbish enough in this very room to heat a rich man's palace for a month!"

Julia pats his hand. "Let's hope it does not come to that, Ulys."

"We shall see."

"We shall." With another touch, one that lingers.

"In truth," he says, "it's worse than you might think. I have lost not just all that we had but all that we had and then some." He relates, in the clearest and most confessional of terms, the story of Sunday morning's fraud. How Ward came here to deceive him when she was out. And how, by deceiving him, Ward deceived Vanderbilt at second hand.

When he is finished, she lifts an eyebrow and says, "Do you see? You should have gone to church."

He knows that she does not mean it entirely. "Good heavens, Julia, the way that Ward told his pathetic story, I imagined that I alone could save the firm."

"That was the way he wanted it. Your intentions were good."

"My thinking was not. And Vanderbilt put his faith in my judgment."

She bites her lip.

"You are not responsible for his investments, Ulys." True or not, she hopes it gives him comfort.

He draws breath. "The check was written to me, and it is I who must repay it." He folds his napkin and rises and goes off to find a cigar, wondering how many of the precious things remain and how he shall manage to do without them.

He has not been reduced to selling firewood from the back of a hay wagon, but he has been brought low in a thousand other, subtler ways. He has given up the family's rented pew at Central Methodist Episcopal for lack of funds. If he attends with Julia, which he does even less frequently now than before, they must sit in the public area or with generous friends. Either course is shameful and shamefully conspicuous.

He has put up for sale various bits of real estate that he and Julia have acquired along the way. One insignificant little house in Washington. Two even less significant little houses in New Jersey.

He has worn out his wrist composing long and passionate letters to every friend and relative and business associate who ever invested a dollar in Grant & Ward upon his recommendation—letters bursting with apology and bleeding impossible promises of restitution. He takes note of the postage that he affixes to each one as a drain upon his dwindling finances, and he silently adds it to his growing mountain of regret.

He has wasted days attempting to reclaim various pieces of precious memorabilia that have made the journey from his house to Buck's and finally to Ward's apartments. Without exception they have vanished into the holdings of collectors—enriching that young devil's pocketbook along the way, no doubt. Grant's name gave the objects their value, but Grant himself is helpless to sell or even recover them.

He has sought—through a legal labyrinth of transfers, deeds, bequests, estate dissolutions, and wills, both contested and otherwise—to sell the brownstone on Sixty-Sixth Street. Julia, thanks to the bequest of some deceased Dent in the faraway past, still owns one little house in the country that would serve them well enough instead, with the added benefit of extracting them from the limelight of Manhattan. In the end, however, they cannot sell the brownstone, because they do not actually own it. Not entirely, so far as anyone can determine. The acquisition of it was just another sham, money traded for the illusion of money, arranged by Ward for his own benefit.

Altogether, the general has spent more hours than he cares to admit in a kind of deadened, defeated, and solitary rumination over his personal failings and the shortcomings of mankind in general. *I have made it the rule of my life to trust a man long after other people gave him up*, he writes in his journal. *But I don't see how I can ever trust any human being again.* In this indictment he might include himself.

Forty Days and Forty Nights

He is Sisyphus in the Adirondacks, toiling up a mountainside under the burden of his own history.

To an outside observer, his efforts would look like either devotion or slavery. He thinks as he goes of the abandoned project in Santo Domingo. He pictures thousands of colored men and women trudging down dirt roads and cattle paths toward makeshift seaports along the edges of the poisoned South, where they wait unawares for transport to another false promised land. Such faith it would require, and what misery, to throw themselves into a poor reproduction of the business that enslaved their ancestors.

He pictures men like Fabens and Cazneau, buying up great tracts of land that might be turned into plantations ahead of settled law. He pictures a second War of the Rebellion fought at an impossible distance and fated to failure. He pictures new generations of colored men and women suffering all their lives long, their plight made invisible by distance.

He pictures, most specifically of all, a second Robert Terrell enchained—enchained and toiling forever, a Sisyphus himself. He would be unlikely to show a timid and accommodating spirit under such circumstances, and for that he would suffer. The whole world would suffer. The man's light would be lost.

CHAPTER 15

1884

Tribute and Transition

Buck has failed every one of them. His wife and children, his sister and his brothers, his in-laws, various members of his extended family both known and unknown, and hundreds of anonymous investors from around the globe.

He has failed his mother and his father most grievously of all, for thanks to their condition in life—their accustomed standard of living, their lack of his father's well-deserved military pension, their incautious accumulation of debt, and their perilously advancing age—they have little chance of recovering. He has unwittingly doomed them, and in so doing he has doomed and disgraced himself.

So he goes to his knees, casting all dignity aside and begging forgiveness that he surely does not deserve. What he deserves is to be denied pardon of any sort, and a part of him fears that receiving it instead might only double his agony.

His mother, of course, bestows forgiveness. "The blame belongs to Ward. To Ward and to Fish, that pair of scoundrels."

He sighs and blinks back a tear.

"They took advantage of you. They sullied your reputation—and your father's."

Buck's mind goes to those two, and from there to every villain who supported or endorsed them. He curses the army of thieves who abetted them at the Marine Bank. He curses the Marine Bank itself, by God, its board of directors and its management, its bookkeepers and its tellers, its depositors and its employees—all the way down to the man who sweeps the floors at the close of each day's business.

His mother wrings her hands and nods, suppressing a tear of her own.

His father does nothing of the kind. His face hardens a little, his eyes narrow a fraction, and his shoulders draw perceptibly back. In an instant he becomes for all the world his old battlefield self, cool and analytical, impervious to doubt and distraction, utterly contained and prepared for the inevitable. "You have gotten it topsy-turvy," he says. "We mustn't lay blame upon the foot soldiers but upon those higher in command."

"Ward and Fish were at the top, not you and I."

"Investors may have assumed otherwise."

"They were duped, just as we were."

"We were incautious, Buck."

"We were deceived."

"And we were imprudent."

"They dragged our good name through the mud."

"And we permitted it, and punishing them will never wash our reputations clean again. Only you and I can do that."

*   *   *

Strangers and friends rally around him in ways both small and large.

The United States Senate offers its inadequate usual, in the form of a bill to reinstate the military pension of which he has been deprived. The legislation would set up a kind of cups-and-balls diversion in which he would reclaim his rank as commanding general of the army and then immediately retire with full pay plus the coverage of substantial expenses. Most Americans would approve of the result without question—set the man himself on a city street or in a town square for a vote by spontaneous acclaim, if you doubt it—but the Senate is not always a reliable mirror of the people. The same bill failed three years before, long before his finances were in ruin, at a time when funding a national hero's living expenses was merely the right thing to do, not the necessary one. Detractors variously claim that the cups-and-balls plan devalues a hard-earned rank. Others suggest that even a demigod like Grant is not beyond the reach of army rules and regulations, however absurd and unjust they may be. At the fringes there are other, more troubling objections as well. You would have to listen hard to find a voice willing to say out loud that Grant's predicament might be the result of his own involvement in the crimes that brought him low, but make no mistake: there are a handful of such whispers all the same, and they carry influence.

Anticipating that the government will do nothing, the nation herself rises to the occasion. Appeals go out in cities and towns from coast to coast, from pulpits and street corners, in private clubs and public taverns, trumpeting subscription plans devised to save the hero of Appomattox. Just one dollar from every man in town will turn the tide. One dollar per man. A penny from any lucky child with that much in his fist. It is every American's duty. Rich or poor, black or white, from the North or from the South. The exercise is of course unsustainable over the long term, but for a while these fundraising efforts prop up both his pocketbook and his spirits.

Then come the individuals. There are not enough to save him— there are never enough of their kind in this world—but their belief in his goodness and their commitment to his well-being are both unshakable. He is like a second father or a favorite uncle or a figure somehow even more precious than that. A kind of laic savior.

The first envelope arrives as he and Julia are sitting down to their simple dinner. They sort the mail as they eat, and inside the first envelope on this particular evening is a letter from a Mr. Charles Wood of Rensselaer County. He seems to be a figure of some prominence in the brush manufacturing trade, and although he has no history of military service—two of his younger brothers belonged to New York's 21st Cavalry, he says, but he was a good deal too old to sign up when the fighting began—he is no less an admirer of Grant on that account. It may be his own inability to defend the Union in person that heightens his desire to do his part today.

Grant would not know him from Adam. Neither would he know his brothers.

Folded into the letter is a personal check drawn for five hundred dollars.

"General," the letter concludes, "I owe you this for Appomattox."

In spite of kindnesses such as this, they have had to let the driver go, and they have dismissed the caretaker as well, along with the gardener and the two maids. Self-reliance is the order of the day. Self-reliance and unaccustomed quiet and a nagging guilt over having had to stop the pay of these longtime loyalists. Terrell endures, Grant's Faithful Harrison, his role as valet growing more general and elastic by the day, but the cook and her helper are gone as well. Julia has unearthed a cache of Jule's old recipes from a trunk in the attic. The ingredients are cheap, the techniques simple, the results unglamorous. They will do.

Sifting through them takes her back to the days at Hardscrabble. Most of them are stained with the very ingredients they call for. They are frustratingly incomplete in most cases, needful things marked by gaps and peppered with corrections and obscured by handwriting that often as not is completely illegible. Julia thanks God that she secretly taught the girl to read, but she wishes that she had taught her to write as well.

Emptied of people, the great house echoes. There is too much space. There is too much of everything. They close off a pair of rooms entirely, draping needless furnishings with disused linens. As the summer comes on, they begin to regard entire classes of possessions with a calculating eye. How many settings of china do they require, after all, and how much cutlery, when dinner is usually just the two of them and a stew suited to a pair of roving cowboys? How many books do they need, when both of them have begun suffering from the fading vision that comes with age? Thus does everything sort itself out into a new kind of order. The extraneous goes into boxes and the necessary remains. For now, at least. There is little sense of loss that goes with the process, until Julia declares out loud the thing that has been in the backs of their minds from the start.

"Who will *have* all these things?" she says.

"*Have?*" says her husband. "Why does someone else need to have them? *We* have them."

"Oh, Ulys." She says his name with a glisten in her eye that is not quite a tear. Not yet.

*   *   *

He goes on foot to a seamy district some miles away and well out of his ordinary rounds, where he finds the shop of a trader in used merchandise. There are other dealers of better repute and closer proximity, but he fears the notoriety that would attach to doing business with them. To let it be known among people of society that President Ulysses S. Grant is selling off his household goods would cause a stir. Better to trust everything to an individual of less visible rank—someone whose customers might think him mad if he claims that these linens, this silver, these knickknacks, once belonged to the hero of Chattanooga. If it costs him a few dollars in differential, so be it. His pride has that much value.

The fellow's name is Quint, and the sign over the transom indicates that he works in partnership with his brother, although the other Quint is nowhere in evidence today. Grant would like to think that one Quint is as good as another, but he cannot be certain and he can only hope—should there be any variation in the matter—that he has drawn the more principled of the two.

This Quint has yellow teeth and yellow eyes and a great scarecrow shock of yellow hair. He occupies a dim corner, seated upon someone else's swivel chair behind someone else's rusty iron desk. Someone else's oil lamp stands at his elbow, but he makes no use of it, for he hates to spend money, having burned every drop of fuel that came in its little tank. He pushes open a curtain to get a better look at his visitor and gapes in awe at the man so revealed.

He leaps upright with a stiff but undisciplined salute. "General Grant, sir."

"Quint?"

"Yessir."

"Which one?"

"*Which one*, sir?"

"Which Quint?"

"James, sir. William's dead." He lets his arm drop.

Grant touches his hat. "My condolences."

"It's been twenty years. He died in the Wilderness."

"Under my command?"

"You ain't to blame. We was just boys. He was a year older, so he went first. I stayed home for a while and got this all started." He sweeps his arm, indicating.

"But he never came back."

"No, sir. Word come when I was boarding the train myself. Our paths might have crossed on those two train rides, but I can't say. One coming and one going. One dead and the other one not dead yet."

"You say William was his name."

"Yes, sir. William."

"God bless William Quint, then. God bless him and God bless his memory."

"Thank you, sir."

"And you're James."

"At your service," he says, permitting himself another rapid-fire salute before they get down to business.

The deal they will strike is square, and Quint will have no trouble keeping his consignee's true identity to himself, and over the coming months they will become as comfortable in conversation as a pair of hardened criminals gone straight. So it is with old soldiers, once the dust has settled. Grant thinks himself lucky to have made the man's acquaintance.

You can find good honest men almost everywhere. Almost.

*   *   *

"How kind of you to make time for an old sinner like me," says Grant as he takes the seat across the desk from William Vanderbilt.

"'An old sinner'? Hardly."

Grant balances his cane between his knees and he fusses with it as if it were a control rod linked to a concealed steam engine that keeps him fired up. He takes no ease in the company of his old friend. Once upon a time, he and Vanderbilt were equals, but that is the case no more. His heroism has turned to ashes. Vanderbilt's wealth, by contrast, goes on and on.

"I'm fortunate that you haven't set a bill collector upon me. Lesser men would have called out a prosecutor, or the Treasury Department."

"If I read the newspapers correctly," says Vanderbilt, "Treasury is busy mopping up the remainder of that young villain's crimes. How many millions of dollars have been lost? How many firms have collapsed? How many men have been thrown out of work?"

Grant looks every inch the rueful old veteran of more wars than should have been necessary. "Too many millions, too many firms, too many men," he says.

"Just so. By comparison, your share in it was a trifle."

Grant scoffs.

"A terrible shame is what it was. Terrible. A good man so near the center of such a thing, victimized like all the rest."

"I am not an especially good man. I am an unlucky one, and perhaps even a greedy one, and most certainly a gullible one."

Vanderbilt appears to consider the idea.

"And being victimized does not absolve me."

"Let us leave absolution to the church," says Vanderbilt. "And forgiveness as well."

"I didn't come here seeking forgiveness."

"I shouldn't think you would, although I'd give it to you if you'd have it."

"No."

"Mr. President, this nation has laid up an enormous balance due with your name upon it. Permitting me to help make you whole would be a small step toward settling accounts."

"I cannot accept anything of the sort. You loaned me one hundred fifty thousand, and you shall have it returned."

"Of course I shall. In good time."

"We must establish a payment schedule."

"By and by we will." Vanderbilt steeples his fingers. "But first, let us consider your condition. Your assets. That house of yours, for example."

"What of it?"

"How much do you suppose it might be worth?"

Grant throws up his hands. "I can't say what its true value might be. Ward worked some of his magic on that transaction as well, you see."

Vanderbilt cogitates for a moment. "Let's say one hundred thousand, then. One hundred even."

"One hundred seems excessive."

"The prestige of its connection to you is worth that much," says Vanderbilt, unmoved. "What about its contents?"

"Certain items are of little value. Others, I suppose, may well be nearly priceless."

Vanderbilt looks pleased as punch. "The good and the bad, then; let's suppose it all comes to another fifty."

"It could. Julia has been spending a great deal on furnishings."

"And a common old campaigner like you wouldn't have been a party to that?"

The general looks abashed.

Vanderbilt draws a little slip of paper from a drawer and marks a number down on it. He scratches his head, puts the pencil away, and finally shows the number to his visitor. "I propose to take title to the house, and its contents, in clearance of your debt. One hundred fifty thousand seems to me a fair price."

"But where am I to live?"

"I didn't say I planned on taking up residence. You'll have the use of the house and its contents for as long as you need them."

Grant sighs.

"This arrangement will get you off to a better start, and it will demonstrate my full confidence in doing business with you."

"That it will," says the general, outmaneuvered.

Vanderbilt will have no more paperwork drawn up on this agreement than he did on the first one. A handshake is all it requires, a handshake and a clutch of expensive cigars thrust into the needy pocket of Grant's overcoat on his way out the door.

Yellow-haired Quint arrives at Sixty-Sixth Street with a little yellow-haired simulacrum by his side—a son, perhaps, or a grandson—and the two are loading cartons onto their wagon when a message arrives for the general. Quint tips his hat to the deliveryman but otherwise does his best to disappear.

"Be quick," he hisses to his little facsimile. "We don't want folks thinking the general is having to move out altogether."

They come once a week, limiting themselves to little surgical visits, hauling away cartons and bundles in small lots so as to make the process inconspicuous. Three sides of the wagon bear the name and nature of

Quint's business, but he conceals them with canvas. He does not need the advertisement, not in this neighborhood. The grandees and swells of the Upper East Side would suspect him of robbery, and Grant would have to come to his defense, and that would be the end of putting a polite face on this desperate project. By the time the messenger's knock at the door has been answered, Quint is freeing the horse from its post and the boy is scrambling up into the back of the wagon.

The messenger bears a note from Fred to his father. Fred has sent it from his apartment across town because he cannot bring himself to broach its subject matter face-to-face. He is in impossible circumstances, he says. Having invested everything he had with his brother's firm, and having lost it all, his finances have reached their limit. He does not hold his father responsible—he is old enough to make his own mistakes and to claim them when he does—but he wonders if the general might see his way clear to helping with a solution. He is thinking of the third floor of the brownstone, where he and his wife and children might . . .

The general needs to read no further. "Mr. Quint!" he calls from the open doorway.

"Aye," says Quint, about to snap the reins and rouse the horse.

"Those last sacks of linens," says Grant. "I think we shall be holding on to them after all."

Forty Days and Forty Nights

Ward troubles him day and night. Ward, who ruined his life and the lives of those around him. That vile stain on humanity's heart is in custody now, and the newspapers report that his wife, through a mazy series of maneuverings, both legal and extralegal, has absconded with his riches. Grant cannot remember the details of it, and he sometimes wonders if the business happened at all. It would be perfectly just if it did, however, and he is satisfied with that.

Yet Ward will not let him rest. He appears in the manner of a revenant, present but not entirely, uninvited but not inexplicable. He is a dead man not dead by any means but ghostly nonetheless. It is the very worst kind of haunting.

If the man desires forgiveness, he shall find none here. The lesson that he taught the general — that there are some acts, and some men, utterly beyond forgiving — came too late. Grant lived most of his life without learning it or having cause to, although he surely had opportunity. His naïveté served him poorly, served his country poorly, and served his family most poorly of all. And he had taken pride in it for a time.

He supposes he might owe the scoundrel a debt of gratitude. Better to learn a valuable lesson too late than never to have learned it at all. Being fleeced by Ward changed his entire life. It made his younger self—boy and man, farmer and soldier, general and president—into a person who would one day lose everything—wealth, reputation, health, self-respect—by the scheming of a cold-blooded little reptile.

He would spend more time and energy hating him if he had time and energy to spare, but he realizes that Ward is only a liability now. There shall be no place for him in the memoirs, which means that time expended upon him is time wasted. He cannot, however, control his dreams.

In one of them he finds himself back in time, to the very day when he delivered his testimony regarding the Grant & Ward affair. He sees the interior of the courthouse in minute detail—the plaster scrollwork in the highest reaches, the grain of the wood in the dark wainscoting, the worn spots carved by men's boots into the steps that lead to the witness stand. He remembers how he blamed himself in his deposition—his carelessness, his gullible nature, his ego—as much as he blamed the two thieving miscreants whose punishment his words were even then hammering into shape. Imagine being condemned in court by the savior of the Union! By a former president of the United States! That would carry some real weight. More weight, perhaps, than any civilized man could bring himself to deliver or receive.

No wonder he was spent afterward. No wonder he vacated the courtroom a changed man, the agony in his throat past enduring and the agony in his soul a thousand times worse. A pair of doctors escorted him home and managed to revive him only with multiple injections of brandy and ammonia.

He awakens from his dream of Ward, calls out with a voice made of dead leaves, and requests that Terrell administer another dose of the same that he might sleep again untroubled.

CHAPTER 16

1884

Work

The children, named Julia and Ulysses after their grandparents, brighten the place beyond measure. Julia is eight and Ulysses is three. She tags behind her grandmother like a loyal puppy and he tags behind his grandfather the same way, and all around they make a heartwarming sight. The children bring so much buoyant happiness into the place that for periods as long as an hour their grandparents can almost set aside the dire reasons they are lodging here.

There is work to be accomplished and there are lessons to be taught and there are futures to be considered. Julia and her little namesake prepare the meals, which becomes an educational opportunity for both of them. Ulysses and his miniature tend a vegetable garden concealed in the space behind the brownstone. They read and read and read. They take long walks in Central Park, where it is possible to observe something very much like nature without the expense of hiring a carriage.

Having Fred and his wife, Ida, on the premises has advantages as well—advantages that go beyond their paying a share of the bills. Ida does most of the laundry and keeps the premises not as tidy as the paid staff did, but tidy enough. She appreciates having the two senior Grants helping to raise the children, and she is always ready to take over when the old folks grow tired. As for Fred, his working schedule outside the house is, shall we say, spotty. There is always something to be repaired around the premises, though, no matter how poorly he may accomplish it. Moreover, he and his father became grand old chums on that world tour a few years ago—little Ulysses was not so much as a gleam in anyone's eye back then—and every time they settle in together for breakfast or coffee, they feel hovering over them the ghosts of old scenes in the elegant dining rooms of hotels and steamships.

It is after a month or so that Fred first encounters the abandoned beginnings of his father's memoirs. He happens upon the general in the library, sitting in an armchair with his chin in his hand and his back to the door, mulling over a handful of loose sheets that bear his handwriting. Fred clears his throat to gain his attention.

"Oh," his father says, with a startled little jump. "Your mother got me going on a little project some time ago. She thought I was at loose ends, perhaps even a trifle bored."

"'Idle hands . . . ,'" says Fred.

"This was back when our finances seemed assured, of course." He gathers the pages into a stack and squares them upon his knee. "These days, I am far too busy for such nonsense."

"And the nature of this nonsense?" asks Fred.

His father shrugs. "A memoir," he confesses. "Something in that line."

"A memoir! What a fine idea!"

"Your mother thought so. I had reservations." He slides the pages into an envelope and rises to place them back in a disused corner of a disused shelf.

"Reservations of what sort?"

"Doubts as to how much demand there could possibly be."

Fred barks out a laugh that surprises them both. "*Demand?* By God, the whole world would want it."

"Alas," says the general, undeterred, tucking the envelope away, "the time for such fancies has passed."

But it has not passed, not at all, and come evening, when Fred slips into the library to assess the work, he is more certain of that than ever.

Fred has connections with a fellow in the publishing business, a certain Richard Gilder, editor of the *Century Magazine*. He visits him in his office the very next morning, intending to raise the question. He has with him, folded in his pocket, the first pilfered pages of the raw manuscript, and he assumes that this modest exhibit—along with his father's good name—will be enough to make the sale.

Gilder is a small man of furious aspect and bristling energy, and Fred finds him at his desk, bearing the aggrieved look of a sea captain charting a course directly into a typhoon. "Forgive me, Colonel Grant," he says, calling Fred by his old rank as he comes around the desk. His hand is extended and his smile is fierce and fixed. "These advertisers seem to believe that they have me by the neck. They put in a little money, and they think they own the magazine and the press that prints it."

"Ha-ha," says Fred.

"They'd tell me what to put on every goddamned page if I let them. But I'm still the editor. The *Century* still belongs to me."

"Ha-ha," Fred says again. "I should say so."

"Don't humor me, Colonel."

"I wouldn't think of it."

They push on through the required pleasantries. There is no likely reason on earth for Fred to be here, so when the essentials are finished, he goes directly to the point. "My father," he says with a meaningful arching of his eyebrows, "has been working on a little project that you might find of interest."

"Something about the war?"

"Something better," says Fred. "Much better. Something about his life."

"I haven't got room," says Gilder.

"You don't have room for General Grant?"

"I don't have room for his *life*. People want war stories. They want battles. Action. Strategy. Give me two thousand words on Shiloh, something nobody's ever seen before, and I'll have it on the newsstands in a month."

"How much?"

"Four hundred dollars."

A theatrical frown from Colonel Fred.

"Four hundred, and I'll commit to taking three more pieces to boot. Three more battles. That's sixteen hundred for the whole ball of wax."

Fred's expression does not thaw.

"He can name his own subjects. Chattanooga, the Wilderness, Appomattox—I'm open to anything he likes."

Fred grinds his teeth.

"All right, all right," says Gilder. "I'll make it five hundred per. But that's strictly out of respect for the general and the kindness of my heart. I'll end up rewriting the damned things anyhow, top to bottom. I always do."

*   *   *

The promise of five hundred dollars is all it takes to get the general fired up about writing again. He feels useful once more, and not like a desperate salesman reduced to peddling his own castoffs via the estimable Quint.

Gilder's orders suit him right down to the ground. "Spend your time on the battlefield," Fred puts it, "not looking into the mirror." The charge frees him to step out of the frame and deliver the unadorned facts with no need for philosophy or opinion. Apparently, his instincts on this point were correct from the start. He could remind Julia of their earlier disagreement on the matter, but he does not need to. She knows everything. She always has. She carries his every thought in her heart, as he does hers. There is no need to emphasize this one in particular.

With a copy of his report on Shiloh open on the desk, he sets to work. His spirits are high, and he is encouraged by the clarity of the assignment. How much easier it shall be to reduce the official reporting to two thousand words instead of manufacturing something new out of whole cloth. It is a matter of leaving out, not putting in. That is as it should be. He works steadily, pausing only for a cigar or a cup of coffee. As the day progresses, the house comes alive around him. From his desk he hears the sounds of his loved ones going about their day. They buoy him up and they carry him along.

The job takes him four days. It comes to three thousand words and a few hundred more, the excess of which he considers a little lagniappe for the *Century* and its readers. A gift from the author, at no extra charge.

*   *   *

"You're certain your father wrote this?" says Gilder, holding it up to the lamp as if hoping to reveal some sort of spirit writing. "It looks too neat for a man of action."

"I copied it out, but he wrote every word. He has a very orderly mind. He is orderly in everything."

Gilder nods and purses his lips. "Shall we have a look, then?"

A brittle smile from Fred. "You don't need to interrupt what you're doing right now."

"It would be an honor," says Gilder, "and anyhow, it's no less than the general deserves." He smooths the papers flat out on his desk and begins.

The sighs and sniffs and throat clearings that emerge from the man over the next ten minutes are dispiriting, to say the least. His expression goes from a kind of dull wonderment to the rawest offense and finally all the way to pure desolation. He gawps. He gasps. He claws at the pages like a starving animal seeking nourishment. And by the time he turns the final page, he is shaking his head like Jehovah Himself mourning the loss of the very last good man in the world.

"Oh, no," he says, as if there is any need to say it. "I'm afraid this will never do."

Fred wavers.

"It's a complete misfire. I could have done the same job by taking a Bowie knife to one of his old field reports. There's no heart in it, no soul."

Fred stammers.

"*There's no Ulysses S. Grant, for God's sake.* What am I paying good money for?"

"But you said—"

"And it's too long, besides. Didn't I ask for two thousand words?"

A sheepish nod from the colonel.

"I thought so." He crushes the papers in one fist, gives them a burn-ing look, and dashes them to the desk. "Don't make me do the cutting, Fred. I'll cut the whole damned thing."

"You'd still owe the general five hundred dollars," says Fred. "You have an agreement."

"Hold me to it, and the world will know your father's failure in this simple matter. I possess a large voice, after all, thanks to the *Century*. Imagine his disgrace."

"Refuse to pay," Fred counters without hesitation, "and the world will know you as General Grant's one and only stone-hearted, gold-plated, cast-iron debtor in his time of need. Imagine *your* disgrace."

Gilder pauses to take a second look at the article. And then a third and perhaps more charitable one. "I suppose there might be something here that we can work with after all," he says. "But I shall have to meet with the general face-to-face. No more middlemen."

"So be it," says Fred, relieved to be a messenger boy no more.

In the general's presence, Gilder is a changed individual. Every inch the gentleman, ingratiating but not unctuous, he becomes for the better part of an hour a courteous expert in one trade offering particles of wisdom to an expert in another. This show of restraint costs him dearly. If he could have accomplished it by means of some potent chemical draft, he would have done so. Instead he accomplishes it by will, and he ends their in-terview with a lump in his throat, a catch in his breathing, and a chilly ring of perspiration saturating his collar.

The general returns home and settles in at his desk, a handful of pages in hand. "This writing is a delicate business," he says to Julia. "More so than I've ever dreamed!" The pages are carefully marked by the editor's hand, and there is a long explanatory note, eloquently worded and respectfully submitted, accompanying them. Julia settles into the chair opposite the desk and considers it all at length.

"You have your work cut out for you," she says at last, rather than saying the thing that is in her mind, which is that she was correct about all this from the beginning. *The facts are known; what people want is the man and his understanding of them.* But what use would there be in bringing that up again?

The general takes the papers back and bunches his lips behind his whiskers. "Frankly, I don't know that I'm capable of doing it properly."

"Of course you are."

He tips his head as if to let a thought come loose and then rights it again. "Clemens could do the job in an hour."

"He couldn't do the job at all. It would sound like Mark Twain when he was done. It wouldn't have an ounce of Ulysses S. Grant in it, and that's what people want."

Grant fingers the letter. "Including Gilder, apparently."

"Including Gilder." She rises to her feet.

"Julia," he says, reflective, "you were right all along, weren't you?"

She drifts off toward the door. "Let me know if I can help," she says. "Until then, I should leave you to your work."

And it *is* work, although it is a different sort of work from any writing he has attempted before. Drafting his old field reports was little more than recitation. Trimming them down into that failed first draft for the *Century* was plain carpentry. This, *this*, is something else altogether. The aim is not just to show the facts but to show the facts as they presented themselves to him in the moment of crisis. If he is to accomplish this, he must somehow admit the reader into his own mind. Not directly, of course—not with all the chaos and turmoil that pass for a man's awareness moment by moment—but in an orderly and more or less linear fashion. He must find the thread in it, the thread that traces the thing's course and establishes its rhythm and suggests its melody. For what is war if not a rising and falling of music—hideous, rackety music played on broken instruments by dying men—from which must at length emerge the resolution that has lain within it all along?

It is easier said than done. It requires writing and discarding and writing again. He gets the largest things wrong and the smallest things right, and he wastes paper in unforgivable quantities given the needs of the day, but he does not believe that he is wasting time. Time is the least malleable and extensible of possessions—it is always more precious than we are willing to admit, even to our secret selves—and although he knows that he is using it, he believes that he is not using it unwisely.

When he is finished, he knows it. He emerges from this second Shiloh with two thousand words in his fist and a clarified understanding in his mind. He has earned both of them by seeing himself not as the only player on the field and not even as the central one but as a single soul of equal weight with one hundred thousand other souls alive and dead on that bloody ground, each one due the same portion of respect. He feels himself a better man for it, refreshed and enlivened.

Julia reads it, and in its pages she sees her husband.

Gilder, gobbling up the manuscript while the general waits in an outer office, has a nearly irresistible urge to write the man a check for five hundred dollars on the spot. He would do it, too, and he would hand it over with a smile and a hearty clap on the back, if only it did not seem so indelicate. Not that delicacy has ever been paramount in Gilder's list of virtues, but still. Something about the general's presence seems to have at least that much of a refining effect upon him.

As for Grant, on the other hand, coming home with five hundred dollars in his pocket would have capped his success. He'd have been Hiawatha returning to his hungry family with a sudden miracle of red deer. But it is not to be. Those days, and that untamed country, are gone forever. So he and Gilder trade smiles and pleasantries as if this transaction were the merest trifle, an automatic thing to be repeated time and again in the coming weeks. Which it surely is. And that will have to be sufficient for now, so far as miracles go.

He debates walking home versus hiring a carriage. His leg pains him still, to a greater or lesser degree, depending on the weather. And he often finds himself a little breathless after a good walk these days, probably thanks to his long love affair with cigars. But in the end, thrift carries the day, and he goes on foot. He knew Vermonters who walked home from Virginia hobbled by greater handicaps than his. He sees that hubris ruled his mind regarding that carriage ride, pure overweening hubris, and he puts it shamefully away. God bless Julia and Fred and Ida; they shall never know that he so much as considered the expense.

Now, add Buck and his wife to that list. For when Grant arrives home, he is greeted by the news that they, too, plan to move in. That makes two sons, two daughters-in-law, and—with precious little Miriam, the youngest of them all—three grandchildren under his roof altogether. This time, since most everything else of an excess sort has already gone to Mr. Quint, the younger Grants shall come complete with their own bedsteads and mattresses, a pair of tall wardrobes, and a chest of drawers.

His house, the general complains in jest, will soon take on the character of a barracks.

"Then you shall feel right at home," says Julia. "Provided you don't mind sharing command with me."

"I have never complained before," says the general.

A good bit later, when the excitement has died down and they are settling into their beds, she remembers to ask about Gilder and the piece describing Shiloh.

"Oh, it was a total success," says her husband. "An absolute victory."

"Does he want modifications?"

"No."

"No?"

"No."

"Bravo, then, Ulys. Bravo."

"What he *does* want," he says as he douses the light, "is the remaining articles. Just as soon as I can manage them."

"Grand. And when you're done, how about resuming your memoir?"

He laughs. "One thing at a time. One thing at a time." The truth is that if he could get away with it, he would light the lamp once more and get straight to work. Straight to work on the whole business.

Forty Days and Forty Nights

His youngest brother, Orvil, is all ages at once—a little boy and an old man and every distinguishable stage in between, as if Grant sees him through some supernatural medium. The clothes upon his back shift and shimmer with his indeterminate condition and they will not stay fixed. He is a tattered ragamuffin one moment and a withered old mendicant the next. Nonetheless, Ulysses knows him. He knows his every particle and pulse, clean down to the atom. The two differed by thirteen years in their youth, and they were separated in adulthood by their opposing constitutions, and they have been separated again by the cruelties of the grave, but it makes no difference. They are brothers yet.

He wonders if they might be on the verge of meeting again, in heaven or elsewhere. If they are to reunite somehow, then he shall surely be reunited with his father and his mother and his brothers and his sisters as well. Why he, the eldest, should have outlived them is a mystery too great for him to comprehend in this condition—whether he is awake now or asleep, cold sober or under the influence of Dr. Douglas's life-sustaining compounds.

He lets it go.

Orvil, staying to the customs he forged in life, wants for money. His need is apparent in his clothing and in his comportment and in his demands. He reports that he has discovered an opportunity certain to make them both rich. The specific nature of it varies from moment to moment and instance to instance. Sometimes it is a railway and sometimes it is a mine and sometimes it is an undervalued stock that will only go up and up in value. Sometimes it is a thing that doesn't register with his living brother long enough to survive into the dreamless world. It is pure and undiluted opportunity, forever out of reach.

He insists that a modest investment on Ulysses's part is guaranteed to grow into a fortune in no time at all. Time is the special gift of the living, is it not? Absolutely. He understands that now. He has learned it the hard way, for these days he is a helpless dead man with no opportunity or agency in this world. His brother Ulysses is all that he has. His eldest brother, who cursed him in life and did not so much as attend his funeral when the moment of his passing came.

They say that Orvil's spirit was broken when he lost everything in the Great Chicago Fire, and he recapitulated that loss again and again along the path of his steep decline, losing his connection to reality and losing opportunity after opportunity and losing one imaginary fortune after another. Ulysses considered it a kindness when he transported him to the New Jersey State Asylum for the Insane, but at this remove he cannot put his finger on precisely whom that kindness served. He fears that it was himself.

I will quit drinking, Orville says, *if you invest.*

I have already quit drinking, he says, *as a token of my resolve.*

He beseeches his brother for the sake of his wife and children, whom he left penniless upon his death.

Grant tells him that he possesses nothing. Only these pages full of words piling up everywhere. In the end it amounts to nothing but memories and ephemera. A man cannot invest such transient things, can he?

CHAPTER 17

1885

Clemens

As if his usual work of filling pages and lecture halls weren't enough, Clemens has lately gone into publishing. He has formed a corporation and hired his nephew to run it, and he has leased an office and laid on a staff. In a month's time they will be taking out *Adventures of Huckleberry Finn* under their own private imprint, a scheme either bold or foolhardy. It may in fact be both. Clemens is a knowledgeable amateur at best—the nephew is less than that—and the project would be certain to lose money if it did not have the name of Mark Twain attached to it. Regardless, he has decided that it is better to be a respectable publisher than to contend with disreputable ones. He's had his fill of them, by God.

Just now he is returning home on a rainy Manhattan night, having spent the last hours regaling a full house at Chickering Hall. His beloved Livy is on his arm, and he holds her close and shelters her beneath a great raven's wing of an umbrella. The man makes a study in contrasts:

Clemens with his black stovepipe hat and his black overcoat, Twain beneath it all in spotless white.

A pair of men step from a lighted doorway and precede them along Fifth Avenue. Clemens takes note because he has lately done business with one of the two. The fellow is in the magazine business, which comes with monthly deadlines and biweekly paychecks—not the book business, where deadlines are rare and paychecks are rarer still. His name is Gilder, and he edits the *Century Magazine*, and Clemens keeps pace but does not reveal himself.

Gilder speaks now to the fellow at his side in a careless and unwary tone, as if they were still in his private office. "What's more," he says, "I'll have you know that General Grant has determined to publish his memoirs. He said so today, in so many words."

Clemens considers what interest a magazine man could possibly have in a project as enormous as the general's memoirs. As enormous and as stupendously profitable. There is money to be made in magazines, but not on that scale. A memoir from Grant would be to Clemens's own upcoming book as lightning is to a lightning bug.

When Livy goes out the next morning, he asks her to please find him the latest number of the *Century*. She does, in a shop nearby, and once he and his cigar have made a study of it, the circumstances become a trifle clearer. This very issue, lo and behold, contains an article attributed to Grant himself, on the subject of the Battle of Shiloh. A note from the editor says that a second article is to be published shortly, this time on Chattanooga, with that one to be followed by another. *Good God,* Clemens wonders, *is there no end of it? Does this pirate mean to release the general's memoirs on the installment plan, at a few pennies an issue?*

He knows the meanness of the man's business practices and the small-ness of his worldview. He knows them firsthand and in close detail. Last month's *Century*, after all, had as its centerpiece three chapters from *Huckleberry Finn*. He chews his cigar and contemplates what a great tightwad Gilder is, how little pay could be pried from his recalcitrant hand for three precious chapters of his own book, and how enormously the circulation of the *Century* was boosted by the inclusion of his name within its pages. He believes he can calculate that last figure to the quarter ounce, and he is confident that he can figure its worth in advertising dollars to the last scandalous nickel.

Oh, Gilder is a cunning operator indeed, and now he means to co-opt the name and reputation of Ulysses S. Grant. Indeed not just his name and his reputation but the work of his very hand, the general's words spilled out like blood in exchange for a few pieces of silver. It is an affront to the nation. It is an affront to decency. It is enough to make Clemens fire up a fresh cigar and set out on foot for Grant's brownstone, not even pausing to take lunch with Livy. He tells her it's an emergency. He advises her to think of him as a cavalry unit on a daring mission to rescue the army's sacred head.

This is not the first time that Clemens has dropped in on the general at home. Rare are the men who would attempt an assault so bold, but Mark Twain is welcome everywhere.

He has good reason to expect to find the general here, now that the firm of Grant & Ward has closed its doors. Stopping to visit him in those offices was always a delight, for Grant seemed to have no real work beyond entertaining a stream of admirers and smoking countless cigars from a humidor that stood near his desk. There were rumors that he was at work on building a railroad line from Mexico City to Guatemala, but Clemens never saw evidence of it. Perhaps the plans were obscured by the thick clouds of tobacco smoke. In any event, the real work of the firm—the manufacturing of wealth in great quantities from out of thin air—was apparently accomplished by his son Buck's partner, one Ferdinand Ward.

All of that is lost now, of course, having been revealed for the sham it was. The company is gone and Ward is gone and the money is gone for certain. Clemens only hopes that Grant thought to retain the humidor.

His knock is answered by the welcoming Terrell, and they proceed to Grant's study. The room has about it a suffocating air of desperation, a gray sense of things coming to an end. The general is seated at his desk, bent over at a slight angle and holding himself delicately, as if in secret pain. Fred stands by the window reading aloud from a sheaf of papers. He trails off when Clemens enters and he lets the papers drop to his side, but the Missourian can tell from the little he's heard that the document is a contract—specifically, a contract for the publication of a book. He knows it by its unsavory smell. There is some relief in that, to tell the truth. At least Grant hasn't been fooled into dribbling his life out in monthly installments to be printed among sentimental poems and peddled on newsstands by the pound. There would be no dignity in that, and less profit.

"You haven't signed, have you?"

"I am just about to," says Grant, taking up a pen. Then, with a mischievous twinkle in his eye, "I've so damned many visitors, I can't seem to get anything done. What did you say your name was again?"

"Clemens," says Clemens.

Grant scratches at his ear with the butt end of the pen. "I thought it was Twain."

"I sometimes believe so, too. It's Twain who writes the books and delivers the lectures, but it's Clemens who keeps the machinery running." He gives the contract a steely look and points at it with an accusatory finger. "You don't need Twain for that," he says. "You need a man of business. You need Clemens."

"All I need is Fred." He beckons his son over from the window. "He and I have full confidence in Mr. Gilder at the *Century*. Besides, I've given him my word. This is a mere formality." He dips the pen.

"The *Century*? May I ask the terms?"

"They are the usual," says Grant, as if he knows what he is talking about, and Clemens's floodgates spring wide.

"*The usual?*" he says. "A figure of your stature deserves terms far more generous than the usual."

"I don't seek charity, and I don't seek generosity."

"You seek to have your pocket picked, then. Let me see."

Grant balks, but Clemens unleashes upon him a torrent of persuasion that proves irresistible. When he does get a look at the contract, he discovers that the terms are an insult indeed. They do not even rise so far as the larcenous *usual*. They are an affront to the usual. Only a highwayman or a thief from the magazine business would dare present them. Such a robber deserves either a hanging tree at sunset or a firing squad at dawn.

Clemens explains these facts as dryly as he can, leaving aside the parts about the hanging tree and the firing squad but making himself perfectly clear nonetheless. When the stormy look that coalesces over Grant's face persuades him that he has accomplished his aim, he gives off. The army has arrived in time to rescue its commander.

But it is not to be, or at least not yet. For the clouds now showing upon Grant's face have gathered not from rage at the miserly Gilder and the threadbare *Century* but from shame at the idea of acting on Clemens's recommendations. "You would not only have me break my bond," he says. "You would have me pauperize a business associate."

Frustrated, Clemens helps himself to a cigar from Grant's humidor—there it stands, thank the God of one testament or another, in the corner by the hat rack—and he offers one to the general while he is at it. Grant demurs. He has given up the infernal things, he says. He has a pain in his throat that they irritate to no end. Clemens may help himself to all he likes, for they are of no further use to him. Clemens knows better—he has succeeded in giving up tobacco a hundred times—so he fills only two or three pockets. He will be returning often enough, and a man must always consider the future.

Once he has worked up some real momentum on the cigar, he explains that Gilder has simply not grasped the import of the book in question. He plans to release it in the way of an ordinary trade publication, simply putting copies out on the shelves and hoping for the best. That might be acceptable for an ordinary book of small interest and little merit, but it will never do for the memoirs of President Ulysses S. Grant.

Grant scoffs. His friend William Sherman's memoirs were published that very way, and he cleared twenty-five thousand dollars in the bargain. Twenty-five thousand!

Clemens draws on the cigar and holds the smoke in his lungs for its calming effect. He must go slowly. He must be patient. Grant is a babe in the woods in these matters. "Sherman was uninformed," he says at last, "and as a result, he made a grievous mistake. He could have cleared ten times as much on the subscription model."

"*Ten times as much.*" Grant's face bears the expression of a man who has just thrown away two hundred and fifty thousand dollars. The expression of a dying man who is leaving his wife and children a birthright of poverty and starvation.

"*Ten times as much,*" says Clemens. "And based upon your name alone, you should clear twenty."

Grant reaches for a cigar, not quite finished with the damned things after all.

Clemens explains that his own upcoming novel—perhaps the general read part of it in last month's *Century?*—is to be published on the subscription model. It is being sold in advance from coast to coast and produced in several grades at various prices. He describes the financial arrangements plainly. He shall be receiving seventy-five percent of the profit—compared against the pitiful ten percent of the cover price that Gilder has offered.

"Seventy-five percent?" marvels Grant. "What sort of company would agree to such terms?"

"One desiring to capitalize on a certainty."

"Nothing is certain."

Clemens shakes his great head. "Now, now, General. As surely as the sun will come up tomorrow, you'll collect a half million dollars from this book in six months' time. And your new publisher will have kept a hundred thousand for himself—fair enough pay for dealing honestly with an honest man."

"But for a publisher to take the risk—at such a modest return . . ."

"Risk? There is no risk. None whatsoever. Not with your name attached."

Grant thinks for a minute. "But I have given Gilder my word."

Good God, the man is incorruptible. Clemens thrusts a finger to indicate the unsigned contract. "Not yet," he says.

"In fact, I am already in business with him, after a fashion. My articles for the *Century*, I mean. We have a relationship."

"If it is an honorable one, he'll be happy to see you decently paid."

"I already get five hundred for each piece."

Clemens doesn't know whether to laugh or cry. Such poor pay, such grievously poor pay, and yet it must be a godsend to the impoverished Grant. "So you get five hundred dollars," he says, "and what does Gilder get in return? Why, he gets five thousand new subscribers every time he sets your name in type." He grinds out his cigar in the ashtray and rises to take his leave, smoothing the knees of his milk-white trousers. He puts his shoulder to Grant and turns instead to his son. "Will you prevent him from harming himself with the nib of that pen until tomorrow morning?"

Fred says that he will.

"You might hide the inkpot."

"That won't be necessary."

"In the meantime," says Clemens, "I shall consult with some publishers I know and gauge their reactions to the prospect. I suspect you'll discover them lined up on your doorstep at sunrise with their checkbooks drawn—just like so many Virginia City gunfighters."

Forty Days and Forty Nights

Reverend Newman finds himself alone with the general. He has not dared hope for such an honor, and he senses something providential in it.

The spring day is balmy, as if the Lord has decided to bless the general with a fraction of the summer that he may not live to enjoy. The windows are thrown open, and the breeze that drifts through the parlor carries with it scents of ancient pine and cedar, bursting dogwood, and green leaves fresh from the bud. The old and the new brought together. Eternity reaching out in both directions.

Ever since breakfast, the grandchildren have been begging for a walk to the overlook by the hotel. You would think they had never seen the world before. The lot of them run free in the woods all the livelong day, but a trip to the civilized realm of the hotel requires adult management. Nellie would take them if there were some other adult to help with the wrangling, but Fred is assisting his father, and the other brothers have gone off to Saratoga Springs with their wives. Reverend Newman is about to volunteer for the duty when he has an inspiration. He ought to encourage Julia to go. It will provide her a little respite.

She agrees, and Fred excuses himself and goes upstairs after a book, and the three of them — Grant and Newman and God — are left to their own devices.

Providence at work, in other words.

The blankets draped over the general move softly in the breeze from the window, and their gentle swaying is the only sign of activity that Newman can detect. Perhaps he is sleeping. There being little time to waste, he moves directly to the man's side. He hesitates for the space of a breath, and then reaches out to touch his shoulder and whisper his name.

The general feels the absence of Julia like an excavation in his heart. She has always been his constant, the two of them inseparable even when separated, but he can detect no hint of her presence now. No singing to the grandchildren. No straightening of his pencils and papers. No soft footsteps in the rooms upstairs. Above all, there is no trace of the scent of her, of her breath or her body or her hair, those things that have long composed the atmosphere of his life.

The only possible explanation is that he is not where he thinks he is. He is still fighting the war, and he is awakening now in some musty tent or requisitioned cabin. Julia is at home with the children. Yes. Absolutely. In his mind's eye he sees her there. He sees her with the little ones and he sees her with that old reprobate and recidivist, Dent — father and daughter reading the newspapers and cheering on different armies, their stubborn prayers doomed to cancel one another out.

The remainder of what he has understood to be his life — his presidency, his ruin, his crippling disease, his desperate attempts to restore his finances for the sake of Julia and their descendants — has been a dream, an illusion, the painful product of his war-torn brain. He is relieved to know that it is a nightmare and not a premonition, for no man could endure the fate that he has conjured for himself.

He feels a tapping at his shoulder and reads it as a signal from the orderly keeping overnight watch. Time to rise. Time to rain down destruction upon the enemy.

When the war is finally over, he shall have his whole life ahead of him.

He ratchets his sticky eyes open a fraction, draws a whistling breath, and clutches at his throat as if to tear it away by main force. Desperate, he casts his gaze around the room until he spies a stoppered bottle and a beaker full of cotton swabs. His eyes roll and redden and he moves his lips but no words emerge.

"The bottle?" says Newman.

Grant nods, opens his mouth, points to his throat.

Newman uncorks the bottle and breathes in its scent. His guess is that it contains alcohol mixed with laudanum or morphine or cocaine or something else on that order. Something whose mere proximity poses a great risk. A compound, in other words, definitely not in the province of a man of his training.

"Have you not got a nurse?" he asks.

Grant shakes his head. Where Harrison may be at the moment is beyond his abilities to communicate.

Newman takes a deep breath of fresh air from the direction of the window, dips a swab into the vial, and peers down Grant's throat as a man would peer off a high ledge into a moat filled with crocodiles. "My God," he says, and then he swallows hard and inserts the swab, as delicately and uselessly as you please, with its tip somewhere in the vicinity of the general's second molar.

Grant nearly chokes. He takes Newman's hand in his own and forces it down another few inches until the medicine on the swab reaches a spot where it can do some appreciable good, and then he holds up a finger to indicate that Newman should hold it exactly there before withdrawing. Five, ten, fifteen seconds go by, and then he nods. The agglomeration clinging to the swab when Newman draws it into the air is unspeakable.

But Grant is breathing more freely, and swallowing with less obvious pain. His mouth relaxes, his shoulders fall, and his wasted frame settles more comfortably into his chair. Newman considers it a modest miracle, a small triumph of anointing, and he credits himself for carrying it off under such difficult circumstances.

The general rummages beneath his blanket for a pencil and a slip of paper. *Well done*, he writes. *Many thanks.* He hands the slip to Newman with a little smile. The smile is genuine enough, for he does not know what he'd have done if he were all alone. He has become so dependent upon others.

Newman accepts the note with a little bow.

Grant writes again. *Julia?*

"Off on a walk with the children."

Grant nods, satisfied, even happy.

While he is on something of a winning streak, Newman has an inspiration. "Have you received the blessings of baptism?"

Grant shakes his head.

"I can provide you with that comfort."

You have given me the comfort I need, the general scribbles. He nods toward the yet-unstoppered vial.

Newman clucks, his brow lowered. He glances furtively around the room in hope of finding some source of water that could pass for holy. A drinking glass. A basin.

Grant, whether or not he recognizes the man's intent, sets his hand upon Newman's. It is no more substantial than a bird's claw, and yet it carries considerable weight. *Stay*, he says by means of a look and a barely perceptible tightening of his fingers.

Newman retrieves the vial with his free hand, covers the top with his thumb, and tips it upside down. Then he sets it back on the table and stealthily puts his hand to Grant's forehead, transferring just a trace of the mysterious liquid. It will have to suffice.

CHAPTER 18

1885

The Agreement

In the morning it is not Terrell who greets Clemens or even Fred. It is Nellie, home from England to lift her parents up in their time of need. And lift them up she does. When word arrived that she was sailing home to New York, her father was so overcome with delight that he was unable to sleep for a week. He is tossing and turning yet.

"Nellie!" shouts Clemens. "How did I miss seeing you yesterday?" Although heaven knows this brownstone could swallow up a battalion and have room left to conceal two or three platoons in the bargain.

"I was at the market with Mother."

"And where is that old rascal Sartoris?" Her husband.

"He has remained in England. Attending to business."

Clemens lifts a shaggy eyebrow just a quarter of an inch. He has heard tales about Sartoris that don't bear repeating under Grant's roof—tales suggesting that whatever business he is seeing to in his wife's absence involves liquor or women or both, with a little gambling thrown in for exercise. He waits a moment and then he lowers the eyebrow like a signal flag, suggesting that the danger is now past and smooth sailing lies ahead. "I should like to live over there one day," he says airily. "The transition between England and death would be unnoticeable, don't you think?"

Nellie smiles. He steps over the threshold, enveloping her in his cloud of smoke. She steps back to let him pass, and he and his vague penumbra drift through the foyer and down the hall toward Grant's study. Nellie watches him as she would watch some beast on the move in its own unfathomable environment. A giant octopus skating above the seafloor, perhaps, attuned to invisible currents, ready at any moment to vanish in a great dark plume of ink. Clemens has always seemed to her this way. He has about him a kind of tentative, unsettled, ghostly air. She has known the man forever—known the tousled shock of hair, the drooping mustache, the merry twinkle of an eye that sees more than you might hope and does not keep its judgments entirely to itself. She has known him always and yet she has never once been at ease in his presence. There is no strict accounting for it. Her father often sees visitors more to be feared than Mark Twain. Armless old soldiers and arrogant industrial tycoons and unintelligible foreign potentates. Half-broken cavalrymen and outlandish representatives of high society and shifty-eyed members of Congress. Not one of them compares.

She draws breath as if she is about to speak and Clemens hesitates, cocks an ear, and turns slowly to sidle back in her direction. Not straight on, but in a general way.

"You caused some excitement around here last night, Mr. Clemens."

"That is my chief business—the manufacture of excitement."

"It had nothing to do with your books."

He flattens a hand against his chest. "You pierce me to the heart, Nellie."

"It had to do with *his* book. *Father's* book."

"The memoirs."

"Yes."

"Is he still bent on giving them away?"

"He and Fred spent half the night exchanging telegrams with a friend in Philadelphia. A friend quite knowledgeable about publishing."

"Every man in Philadelphia is a certified expert on the subject. Ever since Franklin."

"No one in the house slept a wink. Not even Mother. *Especially* not Mother."

"Poor Julia. My apologies. But tell me: This sage from the City of Brotherly Love, what was his counsel?"

"He told Father that you were right."

"About the royalties?"

"Yes."

"About the benefits of the subscription model?"

"Yes."

"About the value of his work?"

"Yes."

"And at no time did he impugn me for a Missouri horse thief?"

"On the contrary. He said you are certain to be Father's salvation. The family's too."

Clemens straightens his back, draws on his cigar, and beams. "I am only returning a favor on behalf of the nation. It's the least I can do."

He parts with Nellie and angles down the hall and steps into the study beneath a cloud of feigned ignorance, making his face a mask of curios- ity and impatience with a hint of woe thrown in for effect. He shall keep his talk with Nellie to himself. Let Grant and Fred report the story in their own way and with their own embellishments. He cannot hear it often enough. He thinks that he shall never tire of hearing it.

They retell the previous night's activities so fully that the part where Clemens is proven right and declared the hero seems unlikely to arrive before suppertime. It does finally come along, though, dragged in like the close of a Russian novel that won't end until a dozen Siberian winters have passed. On the way Fred has traced the logic of their every decision and subdecision and the general has read aloud every word of every telegram. His publishing expert proves to be a newspaperman and therefore perhaps even lower on the scale than the *Century*'s Gilder, but Clemens lets him go without suggesting that he be hanged on general principles. He himself was once a newspaperman, after all. Besides, the fellow has reached a fair conclusion in the matter, regardless of his moral and educational shortcomings. King Solomon could not have done better.

The conclusion reached at last, Grant suggests that they discuss next steps over lunch. He rings for Terrell, who arrives pushing a cart laden with neatly pressed linens and fine china and sterling silver, all of which stand in sharp contrast to the plain meal on offer. Lunch is boiled beans with salt pork, cornbread with no butter, and black coffee minus any kind of sweetening. Clemens has sampled better food in the mining camps, but he reminds himself that sharing any meal with Grant is an honor equal to dining with Julius Caesar. One must make accommodations.

He dabs at his mustache with a napkin and takes over the narrative. Overnight, he says, he was able to consult with publishers both here and in Hartford, the first by means of his own beloved telephone, the other via telegram. The two gentlemen were of identical mind, ready to advance twenty-five thousand dollars against Grant's signature.

"Which of the two would you recommend?" says Fred.

"Oh, they are quite alike," says Clemens. "You should interview them both—along with any others who might be interested. By which I mean every subscription publisher in the hemisphere."

"We wouldn't know where to begin."

"At the beginning," he says. As if there is nothing to it.

The general interrupts, his blue eyes flashing. "We seek your counsel, Clemens. Which of the two would *you* do business with if the book were yours?"

He tugs at his mustache for a moment before hedging his bet. "Well," he says, "the fellow in Hartford was responsible for my last."

"I see. But he's not handling your next."

"No."

"That is not much of an endorsement."

"I suppose not."

"You're publishing that one yourself."

"I am. Well—I am, *after a fashion.*" He pauses and clarifies. "It's actually a new firm, but I am the brains behind it. I am also the pocketbook."

"Correct me if I'm wrong," says Fred, "but are you advising us to do business with a publisher that you won't do business with yourself?"

The truth is that bringing out Grant's memoirs with his own company has simply never occurred to Clemens, and the idea stops him cold.

Fred goes on. "I understand if you would rather concentrate on your own book right now, but these memoirs shall be a year or more in coming. Wouldn't you think so, Father?"

Now it is Grant's turn to be caught on the wrong foot. "Fred," he says, mortified, "don't you suppose that Mr. Clemens would have suggested our doing business together if he wished to do so?"

"I have no idea," says Fred. "It's common to keep a boundary between friendships and business relations. Perhaps he considers the suggestion intrusive."

Clemens clears his throat a bit ostentatiously. "Now that you mention it—" he begins.

"Now, now, Clemens," says the general, raising his palm. "There is no need."

"Oh, but there is. And since the river ice has broken up, I may as well throw in my line."

"Are you suggesting—"

"I am. I most certainly am."

"I cannot permit you to take the risk."

"The risk is nil. The enterprise is nothing but profit, right down to the ground."

"Clemens."

"It is profit and a public service. Any publisher would be foolish not to take it on."

"Please."

"No, sir. I must have the book. Indeed, I *shall* have it." He rises and fumbles about in his pockets until he extracts from their depths—along with an assortment of cigars and crumpled cigar bands and a fountain pen and lucifers both spent and unburned—his checkbook. He places it on the table before him and uncaps the pen. "To prove how earnest I am, I propose that we double the advance."

"Double?" says Fred.

"Don't be ridiculous," says Grant.

"Fifty thousand," says Clemens. "Anything less would be in bad faith."

"It is excessive."

"It is fair. And mark my word, I shall have recovered every penny when the book has been out for a month."

A significant look passes between Fred and his father, but Clemens keeps his eyes on his checkbook and pretends not to notice. There is relief in that look, he thinks, and hope as well.

"Only if you're certain," says the general.

Clemens signs his name to the check and places it facedown upon the desk. "I shall have a contract sent for review," he says, gathering up his belongings and stowing them away in various pockets. "Please feel free to improve upon its wording in any way you like."

Grant is hobbled for the moment by a coughing fit, and he stays behind his desk while Fred sees their visitor out. There is a spring in the colonel's step and a sliver of a smile upon his face.

Clemens decides that he has never done a superior day's work in all his life.

Forty Days and Forty Nights

To judge by the scent that precedes him through the cottage door, Clemens has smoked one cigar after another all the way from New York. That image alone evokes a dense network of memories in the general's brain, a web of actions and possibilities that he shall never again enjoy.

He is reminded of the satisfaction provided by tobacco, for one. How many cigars did he smoke in his lifetime? Countless. They gave him comfort, they helped him think, they provided steady occupation for his idle hands. He spent so much time in their company—and he was so routinely photographed with one gripped in his fist—that a cigar seemed to him and to everyone in the world an extension of his being. It was his sign and his signifier.

He is reminded, too, of the comforts of traveling in style. As a sort of American royalty, he grew accustomed to private railroad cars even more sumptuous than the first-class parlor car lately enjoyed by Clemens. The presidential car would always be the very last in the train, positioned there so as to be as immune as possible to the soot and ash generated by the locomotive.

He is reminded of the company of good-spirited men in motion.

Whether soldiers on the march or horsemen on reconnaissance or a presidential entourage making its stately way through a foreign capital, the atmospheres were always much the same. Clemens no doubt enjoyed that same camaraderie among the businessmen and traveling drummers with whom he made his smoky journey this very morning. Men thrown together into an iron pot and stirred. There must have been dozens of stories told as the travelers grew acquainted and the landscape slipped by—including a few from Clemens himself, no doubt, working up new material for his books and lectures.

Good old Clemens. Kindly old Clemens, with cigars in his pocket and the decency to leave them unlit in the presence of a dying man. It's a thought that leads him right back to his own unrequited love of tobacco, and from there to the niceties of travel, and from there to comradeship among men of purpose, and from there back to Clemens and tobacco once more, and so on, around and around in a narrowing gyre.

Out in the precincts of the conscious world, Clemens cannot so much as rouse him. For an alarming instant he believes that his friend is dead—dead without saying goodbye, dead without completing his manuscript—and he looks around in panic but finds the family unperturbed. Julia is reading a book and Fred is concentrating on some bit of proofreading and Nellie is playing cribbage with Buck, all of them just as cool and unflustered as people long accustomed to sharing their parlor with a dead man. Clemens has seen plenty, but he has never seen the likes of this.

And then, wonder of wonders, the general gasps, trembles violently all over, and forces his eyes open the slightest crack. They are the same old startling blue, if a trifle glaucous. Altogether his appearance is not much improved by his awakening, but, given the alternative, Clemens is satisfied. "Sales of the memoirs proceed apace," he says. "The demand is so great that we have put on new representatives everywhere."

Grant winces a smile in return.

"We have no trouble finding men to knock on doors. Half of the Union Army is lined up to march behind you once more, and a third of the Confederates."

The general's eyes show some fraction of the old twinkle.

"Subscriptions already indicate that our second book—*your book*—will outsell our first by a wide, wide margin."

Grant scribbles on a slip of paper. Huckleberry, *you mean?*

"You have bested my poor orphan already."

The general glances toward Julia, who sits by the window.

Clemens nods once, meaningfully as some old seer, and bends to whisper into his dying friend's ear. "She'll be a wealthy woman, not counting the loss of her beloved."

Grant's eyes brighten, and Clemens straightens up and brushes away a tear. He spies a stack of fresh pages upon the bedside table. The words have slipped from the general like blood. He has shed three hundred thousand of them altogether, and there are not many left to get down.

Put those pages to rest and cover them as you would cover the dead, the general writes upon a little twist of paper.

Clemens smooths the message beneath his thumb, reads it over twice, and takes it for his marching orders.

Grant writes a final note before letting him go. *I will finish in a week.*

"I shall make arrangements to see you then," says Clemens, turning for the door. The New York train does not leave for an hour or two, but he would rather not squander any more of the general's time.

He shall smoke a little on the platform and read the pages on the train as the Hudson sweeps past. If the car contains so much as one other person—and in fact it contains a dozen—he takes no notice. The general is alive upon these pages. Alive and clear-eyed and immortal. Clemens would not dare alter a word.

CHAPTER 19

1885

The Peach

The work goes well, until he dares to eat a peach.

It is evening, and he has put his writing aside. The children and the children's children have gone upstairs, and he is alone in the parlor with Julia. She is reading *The House of the Seven Gables* while he pages through old numbers of the *Century* in search of nothing in particular. The process reassures him that his own articles, which have all been received by Gilder with the same warmth as the first, keep elevated company there.

"Wouldn't you like to read something else for a change?" asks Julia. "It's just you and those magazines."

"They are weightless," he says. "A magazine is ephemeral compared to a book of history or philosophy. I cannot submerge myself in it and lose focus on my own work. And if I cannot sink, I cannot drown."

"There is little risk of that."

"There is more than you might think. I have become prone to distraction in my old age."

"*In your dotage* would be a kinder way to say it."

"Neither way is especially kind." He smiles a rueful smile. "The words are like the circumstance in that way."

Rather than pursue this line of talk any further, she puts her Hawthorne aside and sets out for the kitchen. In a few minutes she is back with a tray upon which are arranged two teacups and a small plate bearing peaches, which she places on the table between them. "Our usual," she says.

"Thank you kindly."

"May I slice yours?"

"No need," he says, reaching for the smaller of the two and taking a napkin to catch its juice. With one corner of the napkin tucked into his shirt collar, he turns the peach in his hand in search of the perfect starting place.

Julia has taken up the knife and is working diligently, cutting away slice by slice.

He chooses his spot, bares his teeth, and bites down. The peach is juicy and delicious for exactly three seconds' time, before his gullet erupts in a paroxysm of agony. He stands up and clutches at his throat, trying to force the bite down, but it will not go. Desperate, he coughs it up and spits it into his napkin and examines it, his eyes running with tears and his throat afire. Coughing, gasping, his body suddenly awash in sweat, he pokes at the wet lump intently but gingerly, as if he expects to find within it some hidden trap.

"Something stung me," he says, half intelligible.

"Stung you? Why, I should—"

He takes a sip of tea to soothe his throat, but it only fuels the fire.

"I'm quite sure it was a bee, or a wasp, or something on that order. In the fruit."

"Ulysses, that seems unlikely."

"A spider, then. Something that set up housekeeping and didn't like my interfering with it." His voice is coming back, but he is still breathless and coughing. Gingerly, he takes another sip of tea. Then he puts the lump of peach back on the plate, and Julia dissects it with her paring knife.

"Nothing," she says.

"Of course not. I've gone and swallowed the blamed thing."

"Perhaps it was a sharp bit of the stone," says Julia, cutting her way to it. But there is no sign of breakage.

"It was assuredly an insect, then." He rubs his chest as though he might be able to detect the thing scuttling about behind his sternum. Who knows what trouble such a malignant little beastie might cause, regardless of how long it might survive under the circumstances? It has poison in it, that much he knows. His throat is evidence.

Dr. Douglas does not like what he sees. He reaches a wooden tongue depressor down to the trouble spot and his patient shivers, his throat convulsing and his eyes filling with tears. Julia stands apart, in the corner, hands clasped to her breast.

The doctor angles an articulated mirror to direct sunlight to the area in question, and he studies the tissues in the vicinity for as long as the patient can tolerate it. When he withdraws the stick, the general collapses forward, bracing his hands upon his knees. He catches his breath, and as he does so the doctor takes his neck in his hands and palpates a knot that he finds there, just below his right ear.

"The good news," he says, "is that it is not some intruder from the animal kingdom, regardless of your inventive theories."

The general attempts a smile. "And the bad?"

The doctor draws a portentous breath. "I fear that it may be serious." The words come out in a hushed whisper. "We shall perform some tests."

"Looking for?"

Dr. Douglas pauses. "Cancer, by the appearance."

"And what is the treatment?"

"We ought to wait for a full determination."

"And should it prove to be cancer?"

Julia winces.

"We shall have some options."

"Options to accomplish what, exactly?"

"To help with the pain."

"Not to retard the disease."

"Most likely not."

"Nor to cure it, of course."

"No. But we shall still have some tools at our disposal."

Grant frowns and looks out the window as if he has spied something of great interest. Perhaps it is the world with him no longer in it. He turns abruptly back to the doctor. "How long, do you suppose, before it kills me?"

Julia gasps.

"Let us wait for a full diagnosis. In the meantime, I can give you something for the pain." He withdraws a cotton swab from his case and wets it with something from a little corked vial. Morphine diluted with water. "Open up," he says.

*   *   *

The general has seen men's arms and legs sawn away with the help of morphine, and he has heard stories of men who've come to depend upon the stuff to go from one day to the next, and he knows the fiddle tune called "Soldier's Joy" by heart. Experience has taught him that in the clutches of war a man will often compose an ode to his beloved, even one as faithless as this.

He employs the treacherous stuff sparingly, allowing himself no more than two doses per day. Otherwise it might cloud his mind too much. When he feels that he needs relief, he resists, and when the pain reaches nearly intolerable heights, he resists still, and only when he is in such agony that he can no longer work does he permit Julia to apply a dose. With the doctor's permission he tries cutting it with gin to minimize its addictive and mind-altering effects, but the resulting compound proves of little use. So he soldiers on—day by day, dose by dose, word by word.

He visits Dr. Douglas frequently for attention to the wound, and on one early visit, after the pain has been dulled with morphine, the doctor dares take a sample of tissue. The open wound has suppurated, and what he extracts is marbled with pus and blood, but he obtains enough tissue that it can be tested by a colleague who has developed some new theories and techniques regarding the matter.

The results are not unexpected, but they are no less terrible for that.

Grant flings himself into his writing more furiously than ever, for work consoles him in any number of ways. The deep concentration can sometimes block out a fraction of his pain. The need to sink into the past and relive it serves to remove him temporarily from the woes of the present. Most importantly, the entire project speaks to him of salvation. Not the celestial kind, but the kind that has to do with atoning for one's mistakes, paying one's debts, and securing the future of one's family. He has made a terrible ruin of his life and theirs, and these unfinished memoirs are his only means of setting it all right.

Clemens has said it shall be easily accomplished—easily and inevitably, once the work of composition is done. May God bless the Missourian for his confidence, if a God there is. The question will have to remain unsettled in this life. He will learn the answer in the next, though, which promises to arrive—or fail to arrive—soon enough.

So onward he toils, his mind racing his body toward a point as yet unspecified.

Forty Days and Forty Nights

He is carried along these days by determination and hope. Determination and hope and whatever chemistry Dr. Douglas might see fit to hazard on any given day. Medicine, like war, is always and ever an experiment. In any event, certain that he will not be granted his customary threescore and ten, the general carries on with all possible speed. Given sufficient effort and fair enough fortune, he will complete his work and send it on into whatever world it might encounter. A world where his wife and children shall live without want, God willing. A world where his shortcomings shall be forgiven.

Beyond that, he imagines some glorious impossibilities.

A world where Jule might one day bless his memory with a single heartbeat's worth of understanding. A world where Robert, whose father was a valet to one president, might grow to be an esteemed counselor to some other. A world where the hostilities that he once believed settled might be settled for good.

A praying man might go to his knees for these things.

He can barely lift his pencil.

* * *

They are as omnipresent as the Almighty, as insistent as a choir of angels.

Black women and black men. Black youth and black children and black babies.

They mass around his bedside. They crowd a strangely limitless and kaleidoscopic space that is all of his life's important locations at once: this cottage, the White House, a campaign tent somewhere in enemy territory. They blanket the high forests and the city streets and the blood-soaked battlefields.

They have a claim upon the whole world.

They have come by the generation—men and women materialized not just from the present but from a past that reaches back to Virginia and to Africa and all the way to Eden. He sees the enslaved, suffering in captivity, and he sees the kidnapped, chained in the putrid bellies of ships. He sees innocent men and women upon distant shores, decades and centuries gone, the lives of their descendants unknowable to them and their own lives unknowable to him.

From here at the end of the world, he sees that he has used these strangers as a man might use a team of mules. He has relied upon their calculated value—not in heart and soul but in dollars and cents—to undermine his enemy. He has taken advantage of their plight, their eternal human plight, to serve a mere nation, a nation that judges him a saint but does not know the content of his heart.

He behaved more humanely toward his enemies than toward these. The Confederates—his brothers after all, fellow soldiers and sons of West Point—he fought and forgave. These strangers, on the other hand, he used and then released—unacknowledged and unprotected—into a treacherous land poisoned with bitterness and defeat.

He dares not hope that they might forgive him.

He hopes only that they will release him when his time arrives.

CHAPTER 20

1885

Faith

The Reverend Dr. John Philip Newman has found Grant a difficult customer for years. Brought into the family's universe by Julia—like certain other unworldly creatures, he will never cross a threshold uninvited—he has tried again and again to bring the fellow around. Capturing the general would mean putting his fame to work on God's behalf. Imagine the possibilities! No matter what subject should interest a fellow like Grant—the outcome of the Saltpeter War, King Leopold's butchery of the Congolese, the secure transatlantic shipping of the Statue of Liberty—with the backing of the general and the help of the newspapers, Newman could conjure an army of right-thinking, hard-praying Christians to get the job done. He could move mountains.

Alas, the man will not budge. Those who should know describe him as faithful but not religious. A good Christian but not a praying man, as if there were no contradiction in that. So far as Newman can establish, the fellow has not even been baptized. He certainly makes no claim to it, and there seems to have been no detectable religious component to his upbringing. Continuing the family custom, he has attempted to raise irreligious children of his own—and he would have succeeded if not for the good and contradictory offices of their mother. Without Julia, the entire family would go to ruin.

Now, however, the diagnosis of cancer has opened up a world of possibilities. Mrs. Grant requires Newman's presence in the Sixty-Sixth Street house at an increased frequency for purposes of comfort and healing, although as a rule the healing is conducted at second hand. They pray over the general every morning, most often from an adjoining room. He assures her that the work is no less powerful for the distance, heaven being at a vast remove to begin with. And as busy as the general might be, the Almighty can surely accomplish His work without the man's help.

Nonetheless, he is now and again admitted to Grant's sanctum sanctorum, provided the general is in a tolerant mood and at a stopping place in his work. At these moments the general tolerates his ministrations or seems to. Newman half wishes that he could open his eyes during prayer to see if Grant is cooperating—on a number of occasions he can swear he hears the turning of a page from the general's direction—but he dares not. It is of no matter. Julia's frame of mind definitely improves as a result of these sessions. And God's work goes on.

Newman hates witnessing the general's deterioration, and he resolves to do something about it. Suffering is God's will, of course, but the arc of God's will can sometimes be diverted, God willing. So he arms himself with all his spiritual resources, and he prays for guidance, and by and by he develops a plan.

*   *   *

He goes straight to the newspapers. People the world over are hungry for knowledge of the general's condition—they are starving for it, by all reports—and no one has more ready information on that subject than he. The doctors, sphinxes that they are, will part with precious little. Thus, he must do his duty regardless of the cost. He may grow famous in the process, but never mind that. It is of no consequence.

There is hardly a newspaper in the city that will not see him and carry his reports, and there is hardly a newspaper in the world that will not reprint them for the good of mankind. A steady stream of information there proves to be, for he obtains new insights into General Grant's condition on a daily basis. He issues a statement of double length and triple intensity on Saturdays, so that those who have been unable to give the general's plight their full attention during the week may spend time on the Sabbath catching up. *After worship*, he hopes.

He insists to the reporters that each story printed must finish with a plea for prayer on the general's behalf, and in so doing he musters his army of souls.

He has critics, of course. Grant himself privately says that he endures Newman's ministrations strictly because they make Julia feel better. Senator Chaffee, Fred's father-in-law, tells reporters, "There has been a good deal of nonsense about Newman's visits. The truth is that the general allows him to pray in his presence only out of kindness. He would hate to wound the man's feelings." Clemens, as could be expected of a man of his inclinations, is the most dismissive of all. "This reporting corresponds precisely with Newman," he insists to anyone who will listen. "It is unadulterated gush and rot, as unbelievable as the man himself."

In any case, Newman's scheme soon bears fruit. Confidently as you please, and with only a trace of that most forgivable of the deadly sins, pride, he announces in press briefings and from the pulpit that Grant is now sustained in life exclusively by the prayers of the people. Thousands upon thousands of prayers. Hundreds of thousands and more. They rise into the atmosphere like fountains, lifting the general up and suspending him in the gracious light of the Father, the Son, and the Holy Ghost.

It is truly a miracle. When asked, he says that he takes no more credit for it than any other man engaged in the effort. His humble voice is just one of thousands, each one called forth by God to do His bidding. Silence him, and the work would go on—no matter what that damned Clemens might think.

Forty Days and Forty Nights

He is nearly beyond the pain.

The work is just now finished, which brings such relief that he could actually go on living for a while, had not the loss of purpose unwound his mainspring. Absent that motive power, he collapses like a marionette unstrung.

The family shall go on without him. Their future is secured. Clemens has promised it.

The general puts down his pencil and vows that he shall pick it up again only to communicate with those he loves. That includes Faithful Harrison, of course. But he is finished with Dr. Douglas. He is finished with Reverend Newman. He is finished with well-meaning visitors. And he is surely finished with the reporters gathered outside like Confederates in the woods, lurking behind trees and concealing themselves in the undergrowth, awaiting the profitable word of his demise.

Where he has hidden this fistful of treasures, no one shall ever know, but he produces them like a conjurer with one last surprise up his sleeve. They are powerful totems: his gold wedding ring, a single lock of a child's pale hair, a sealed letter to Julia.

The ring was consigned to a bureau ages ago, when it ceased to fit upon his finger. It saw him through the war and it saw him through the peace that followed, but it did not see him through his years in the White House. Blame it on too many sumptuous state dinners. Blame it on countless hours behind a desk. These are not proper pastimes for a man accustomed to hardship and action—to field rations and days on horseback—and they took their toll. The ring was last seen in the brownstone on Sixty-Sixth Street. Never mind that. It is here now.

The lock of hair belongs to Buck, but by its color it could belong to any angel whatsoever. By way of identification it has only his initials on the reverse of its paper mounting. The little pinned-down curl could have any number of meanings. In its anonymity it could stand for Ulysses's love for all of the children. It might, on the other hand, signify his enduring love for poor Buck in particular, in spite of that damnable business with Ward. Most likely, in allowing Buck to stand in for the rest, it means both of these things at once.

The contents of the letter shall remain unknown. The envelope reads *My Dearest Julia*, the words written in the same determined, confounding hand with which he composed the final chapters of his memoir. The letter within may be a recent composition, or it may be a testimony composed previously for use in such a case as this. It may be some aggregate of the two, written over the years and just now brought to its final perfection.

A lifetime in a few pages.

My Dearest Julia.

*　　*　　*

He communicates through his vitals now. His state and his state of mind can be interpreted only through diagnostic instruments.

There is little enough left for him to describe or explain. He has communicated almost everything that is in him, and any scraps that might remain require too much effort. The very last syllable he will say aloud is "No," and there will be no truth in it. Fred will ask if he is in any pain, and rather than write out an explanation with his weakened wandering hand and a paper that won't lie flat and a pencil that possesses a mind of its own, he will gather his strength and croak out this one last negation. "No," he will say, rather than trouble anyone with the truth. He cannot bring the curtain down on anything short of reassurance.

During the final day and night, his pulse goes from slow and weak to rapid and irregular and from there to various states in between, all without order or reason. His temperature sinks and rises and sinks once more. Harrison works full-time just adding and removing blankets, opening and closing windows. Dr. Douglas keeps vigil in the hall. Julia does not stir from the bedside. The children come and go.

Along about midnight an injection of brandy seems to help. Encouraged, Dr. Douglas follows it a few minutes later with another, but the general seems as a result to lose as much ground as he has gained. Douglas makes no further attempt and hopes that he has done no harm.

Julia prays and waits. She speaks to her husband from time to time. She sings to him snatches of the old, comfortable songs. Lullabies and love songs and hymns — they are all the same now, they are all one, for they have been distilled and purified into the sound of her voice. She holds his hand all through the night and releases it only when he is gone — releases it to replace upon it the gold ring that she gave to him so long ago. It fits his diminished finger as it would fit the finger of a child.

Fred rises and goes to the fireplace and stops the mantel clock at eight minutes past eight. The second hand has no doubt moved a fraction in the interval between his father's last breath and the touch of his finger to the pendulum, but so be it. Into that infinite unmeasurable gap may the man's soul be released.

How many years has he lived upon this earth? Sixty-three and a trifle more.

How much will he weigh when they carry him out? Ninety pounds and a trifle less.

What has he left behind? A testament.

CHAPTER 21

1885

Processional

The nation weeps together, but Julia weeps alone.

She will return home soon enough, but for now she remains at Mount McGregor. Her only company is Harrison Terrell, sitting stunned on the porch, and Sam Willett, gathering his possessions with the reluctance of a castaway loading his things onto a raft of questionable seaworthiness. The whole world is silent. Even the insects in the undergrowth and the squirrels in the trees and the birds in the air have been stilled. Perhaps they, too, have gone off to New York for the obsequies.

Having lived through a private funeral just days prior, she lacks the strength to attend a public one now. Her absence will be remarked upon by some, but most of the attention will be on the dead man and the pageantry. Julia has no use for the pageantry, because she has no use for anything but the man.

*　　*　　*

In life the general was without pretense, but the spectacle gotten up to mark his passing would suffice for three ordinary presidents, a half dozen kings, and a joint session of Congress. One and one-half million souls have arrived to jam the streets, avenues, boulevards, sidewalks, alleys, parks, rooftops, fire escapes, social clubs, jails, dining establishments, concert halls, hotels, churches, and taverns of New York. Even the brothels and the gambling parlors are tested to their illicit capacity and beyond. Altogether, three hundred thousand men, women, and children will pay their respects at the open coffin. The line of mourners stretches for miles and takes a half day to pass.

Grant's flag-draped coffin travels upon a tall gleaming catafalque as dark as night, drawn by twenty-four identical black stallions and accompanied by an honor guard. This breathtaking assemblage proceeds from City Hall to Riverside Park with the stately inevitability of the apocalypse. In its wake comes a carriage bearing the family, and in the wake of that comes another bearing President Cleveland. Their passage is witnessed from every window in every building along the route, no matter how high. The very trees that line the streets bow down under the weight of men and boys straining to catch a glimpse.

The crowd contains representatives of every race, class, occupation, and locale. Rich and poor, Northern and Southern, Union and Confederate, black and white—all are alike in this time of grief, for all have been laid low the same. As if to signify this brotherhood, a place of honor goes to the 5th Virginia Regiment Band, once part of Stonewall Jackson's brigade. Having been allowed to take their instruments home from Appomattox, they have unburied them now from closet and trunk, polished them up to the highest sheen that age will allow, and reassembled their formation here as best they can, death and disability notwithstanding. A number of positions go vacant now—a bugle in the third row, a flute in the first—where obstinate Southern loyalists have refused to grace the proceedings. It is in their rancorous absence that the old hostilities immortalize themselves.

The general's temporary tomb is itself a kind of miracle, having sprung up nearly overnight. The men in charge would have built it high enough to challenge Babel if they had been given the time. Just beyond the little hill where it stands, the waters of the Hudson are crowded with warships, all primed to mark the occasion with a cannonade greater than any heard during the war. Their aim would seem to be making sure that the general, wherever he has gone, hears the eruption and knows himself bid farewell.

Ulysses Jr.—Buck—climbs down from the family's carriage and takes his place before the tomb, where he waits at attention. He has promised his mother that he shall be her eyes and ears. The intensity of his concentration works to inscribe every moment upon his heart, and for the rest of his time on earth he will be able to summon up the day whole—just as his father conjured those indelible scenes from Vicksburg, Shiloh, and the rest. Such will be his curse and his blessing.

Better to be burdened with this than by the other obsession that has long occupied his mind—that terrible series of events that began with his introducing his father to Fish and Ward, and ended with the general's last desperate charge into the valley of the shadow of death. Even now, as he stands between his brothers and looks out over the throng, he believes that he can make out a hint of that old treachery. It is right there before him, just across the street. An elm tree in full summer leaf, with one solitary figure half-concealed among its leaves.

Ward.

Ward in the flesh.

The disgraced and degraded Young Napoleon of Wall Street, plainly attired and wearing a slouch hat pressed down nearly to the bridge of his nose.

No. It cannot be Ward. It is impossible. Ward is confined in the Ludlow Street jail, awaiting his trial.

And yet there is something familiar about the man up in the leaves, perched there like old Zacchaeus in the sycamore tree, straining to see his savior. There is something about his dimensions and his posture and the jut of his chin. The intensity of his shaded gaze bears something that looks like triumph.

Buck leans back and whispers to a member of the honor guard, "That fellow in the elm. Bring him down and hold him." But the crowd proves nearly impenetrable, and when the soldier has reached the tree, the intruder has vanished.

Whoever he is, at least he has not tainted this sacred day by bearing full witness. Buck is glad to have done that much for his father, even at this extremity.

POSTLUDE

Manhattan

Alongside the river a high tangle of scaffolding has arisen, a framework marking out the location of his tomb. It will be the largest mausoleum in the country, a kind of American Taj Mahal.

Grandeur aside, she is mainly glad that her husband will still be within walking distance of Sixty-Sixth Street. Travel is difficult now, but a good walk is essential. Walking keeps her bones moving. It clears her head and warms her heart. She often walks with one of the children, and occasionally with one or two of the grandchildren. These are family outings of the sort that she and Ulys used to arrange back in the difficult times, along the trails and in the grassy fields of Central Park. Those surfaces are treacherous for a woman of her age, and she keeps to the sidewalk now.

Strangers recognize her as they pass, gentlemen lifting their hats and ladies dipping their chins. *It is the general's widow, still ornamenting these streets thanks to her husband's success in prosecuting the war and getting it down in that book of his.* They know her only as far as she has been il-luminated by his light, a shortcoming that her husband would detest.

To children on the street she is a cipher, not even a curiosity. They know nothing firsthand of Ulysses S. Grant, not the president and not the general and not the man. He is a name in a list, a picture in a book, a story once told and now nearly forgotten.

How poor these children are! How incomplete their education, how limited their understanding. And they are but a single generation on. As time goes forward, this precious present will turn from memory into his-tory, from history into legend, from legend into dust—and no Taj Mahal will slow the decay that has already begun.

If convention and back trouble would permit it, she would bend down to these children and raise them up, one by one, in her arms. She would show them the scaffolding by the Hudson. She would indicate the brownstone still belonging to the family on Sixty-Sixth Street. She would present to them an entire city once occupied by mourners.

She would embrace them with all her unexpended passion, and she would tell them everything that they ought to know.

AUTHOR'S NOTE

There is no such thing as a voice from the past. The moment a writer places one word into the mouth of a person sufficiently dead—George Washington or Joan of Arc, Cleopatra or Adam—he has slipped free from the world of facts.

But there are riches to be gathered out there. The life of the mind is all interpretation, anyhow. We understand the hearts and minds of our loved ones not by the use of some analytical recording device but by genuine moments of attention, imagination, and sympathy. By the same means we can appreciate the hearts and minds of those who came before us—particularly if they've left behind the indelible marks of their character.

So it is with *The General and Julia*. I only hope that I have done justice to the souls both great and ordinary that you'll find in its pages.

ACKNOWLEDGMENTS

This book wouldn't exist without the help of Marly Rusoff.
Its author wouldn't exist without the help of Wendy Clinch.